PRAIRIE PRESTIGE

PRIMROSE SERIES
BOOK SEVEN

TANYA RENEE

Serenade Publishing

www.serenadepublishing.com

For my dad, forever a cowboy and to the memory of his beloved horse, the real Prairie Prestige.

ALSO BY TANYA RENEE

Primrose Series

Prairie Sky

Prairie Nights

Prairie Fire

Prairie Hearts

Prairie Sound

Prairie Rain

Prairie Prestige

Prairie Roads

With The Band

Finding Direction

Love Notes

On The Edge Of Forever

PROLOGUE

Grace Kasper tiptoed into Mary Jane's bedroom, approaching her 13-year-old granddaughter sleeping soundly, a stuffed horse under her arm, her face angelic cascaded by the moonlight streaming through the bedroom window.

Taking a seat on the edge of her bed, she placed a loving hand on her granddaughter's shoulder, leaned in and whispered softly, "Wake up, MJ. It's time."

MJ's eyes fluttered open, and a soft groan escaped her lips as she raised her head off the pillow, groggily trying to focus her gaze on her grandmother as she asked, "The baby's coming?"

"Yes, pretty girl, Pixie is in labor." Her grandmother said with a soft smile. "If we hurry, we can see the baby being born. Grandpa is already in the barn, so throw on your jacket, and your boots are already at the door."

Rising from her bed excitedly with all thoughts of sleep diminishing with the words, "baby coming," she hurried down the staircase, towards the door, grabbing her flannel jacket from its hook and slipping her bare feet into her barn boots. Following closely behind, her grandmother grabbed a stack of old towels, and they sprinted across the yard towards the horse barn. Entering the old shed row barn, MJ made her way to Pixie's box stall and peeked over the gate to see her grandfather, Gatton Kasper, on his knees next to their Arabian Mare. Pixie was lying on the bed of straw, her grandfather's hands running softly over the belly of the laboring horse. Her Grandfather looked up from where he was crouched down, met MJ's gaze, then drifted over to her grandmother with uneasiness in his eyes.

"The baby is breech, and she's too far along for us to call the vet," he said simply as he turned his attention back to the birthing mare. "I'm going to have to help her get the baby out."

MJ glanced towards her grandmother, her face full of concern as she reached for MJ and put an arm around her with reassurance.

"Grandpa is going to do his best." She said with apprehension in her eyes as they watched the back hooves appear, the back legs coming out slowly on a contraction. Her grandfather repositioned himself behind Pixie, reaching inside the birth canal of the mare to carefully help the hind end of her foal ease out, trying not to dislocate the foal's hips in the process and mindful of not pinching the umbilical cord. MJ watched with wide eyes of uncertainty as her grandmother glanced down at her, giving her a melancholy smile. Immediately MJ understood how incredibly difficult this situation was without a veterinarian present.

"Grace and MJ, come in here and help me." Her grandfather requested with his teeth gritted and a firm hold on the foal. "MJ, I want you to crouch down beside Pixie and rub her back and belly, to keep her calm. Grace, I need you to be ready for the baby when it's out."

Both entered the box stall as instructed, and MJ knelt beside the panting mare. Her eyes met Pixie's large dark orbs looking panicked and fearful. "It's okay, Pixie girl, your baby is almost here." MJ said in a soothing tone as she ran her hand over the damp surface of the mare's coat.

Her grandfather gave her a quick nod of approval as he tugged, coaxing the foal out slowly, inch by excruciating inch. Pixie let out a cross between a grunt and whiny and MJ could feel her muscles working hard under her palm to give birth to her baby.

"Almost there, Pixie. You will be a mama soon." MJ said, and with her words, Pixie's head lifted, and she tried to rise only to fall back in a roll, knocking MJ backwards into the corner of the box stall.

"Are you okay, pretty girl?" her grandmother asked with concern.

Nodding, MJ watched her grandfather pull, his grip firm on the newborn foal. With the rump out, the torso of the foal appeared and then with some careful manipulation and confidence that nothing was obstructing the neck and head, with one more strenuous tug, her grandfather fell back with a thud. Covered in fluid, blood, and mucus, he held the newborn foal covered in the membranous sac in his arms.

Her grandmother scooped up the foal, laid it on a towel, freed it from the sac, and, taking a towel, they watched anxiously as her grandmother removed mucus from its nose and mouth and started rubbing it vigorously to revive it. "It's not breathing, Gatton," her grandmother choked out after a minute, her voice thick with worry. "I sure hope we don't have a stillbirth here."

"Lay it on its side and try clearing its mouth and nose again," he suggested. "It may still be with us; we just need to coax it to take that first breath."

Remembering a video she had seen before, MJ rose to her feet and walked over to her grandmother trying desperately to revive the foal. Putting her hand on her grandmother's shoulder, she asked, "Can I try?"

In dismay, her grandmother shifted aside as MJ knelt and positioned the foal's neck, elongating it. She leaned down and breathed into its nose, counted to three and then did it again as her grandparents, frozen in place, witnessed their granddaughter attempt to resuscitate the foal.

"It twitched." Her grandmother said with widening eyes as the legs of the foal moved and its chest heaved in a shallow breath. MJ looked up at her grandparents, and her grandmother asked, her voice filled with awe, "Mary Jane Kasper, where did you learn that?"

"YouTube," she replied, sitting back to catch her breath as she wiped her mouth with the back of her hand.

"Damn, internet is good for something." her grandfather chuckled as he turned his attention back to the mare and his thick brows furrowed with worry, "Grace, run to the house and call the vet, we have a lot of blood here."

With a nod, her grandmother sprang to her feet and rushed out of the barn towards the farmhouse.

Her grandfather sat back on the bed of straw, glancing at the foal awkwardly trying to sit up on its chest. His gaze drifted to MJ, with so much love, pride, and admiration in his eyes as he suggested, "Why don't you name him?"

MJ grinned, then squinted in thought, as she remembered how the names of the sire and the mare were often merged in her grandfather's Arabian horse magazines. With this colt's sire being Desert Prestige and his mare being Prairie Pixie there was only one name that seemed fitting. "I want to name him Prairie Prestige."

Her grandfather smiled proudly as he said. "A perfect name for your first horse. Consider him yours."

CHAPTER 1

It was now or never; this nightmare would finally be over, and she would be free. Mary Jane Kasper grabbed the last box of her belongings and took one last lingering glance at her childhood bedroom, the memories of this sanctuary painting a faint somber smile on her lips. Turning, she rushed down the wooden staircase towards the front door of the old farmhouse. Reaching for her coat, she turned, closing her eyes for one self-indulgent moment. She could almost hear the echoes of laughter and smell the sweet apples, rich pastry, and spicy cinnamon from the kitchen as she played gin rummy with her grandfather while her grandmother baked her famous apple pie.

"I'm so sorry." She breathed out, her words getting strangled by emotion. Picking up her last box of belongings, hot tears pricked her eyes as she turned, opened the front door, and caught her shoulder clumsily on the doorjamb. She winced at the pain still there from the deep bruises that dappled her skin under her clothes. A blunt reminder of why she had to leave now. Chet would be home from the oil fields in a week, and she was not about to be his punching bag again. She was done with his control over her. It was time to let go of this place and start her life over. The further away from Chet, the better.

It had not always been this way. Having met Chet in her senior year of high school, she thought he was incredibly handsome, charming, and sweet. He doted on her, and when her grandparents passed away in a tragic car crash four years ago; he stayed by her side, consoling her the way a committed, loving boyfriend should. Shortly after her grandparents' sudden passing, with no other family and few friends left in town, having Chet move in seemed like the next logical step. He promised to take care of her financially, her grandparents having left her the property and little else. So, with his promises and dreams of building a life with her boyfriend, he moved in.

That's when things changed. It started when he took a job in the Alberta oil fields, going up north to Fort McMurray for weeks at a time, coming home tired and foul-minded. He would blow up at her, get angry, tell her she was useless while he worked so hard to give her the life she wanted. Soon his anger came out in more than just words, and the first time he gave her a black eye, she knew the man she loved had sold his soul to the devil. For three excruciating years she endured his beatings, abuse, threats and slurs, staying only because she couldn't abandon the memories of her family farm. The only home she knew and the only thing she had left from her grandparents. Other than her beloved horse Prairie Prestige, of course.

It wasn't until she found Chet in the horse barn one morning, drunk, a shotgun in his hand, threatening that he would shoot her horse if she ever left him, that she knew she needed to figure a way out.

Over the following six months, while Chet was away, she spent every spare moment fixing up her grandfather's old truck and horse trailer, grateful for all the times she had watched him tinker with it. She sold off scrap metal and machinery her grandfather had stored, knowing Chet had no interest and would not be looking for it. All the money she was able to raise she hid, as she stayed under the radar as best as she could, biding her time till she could make her escape and end the nightmare that had become her life.

The time was now upon her as she lifted the tarp covering her belongings and set the last box down, covering it quickly and securing it with the last bungee cord. Double-checking the hitch, she pulled out of the machine shed and looked around the yard. She knew full well Chet wasn't going to come home, ambushing her, but the paranoia that he might was overwhelming and made her head spin and heart beat out of her chest. The property situated on a quiet gravel road, and with the only neighbor over a mile away, she was confident she could stealthily take the backroads around the town and go undetected. As far as anyone would know, she had disappeared into thin air without so much as a trail as to where she had gone.

Carefully backing the truck and trailer towards the horse barn, she rushed inside to Prairie Prestige's box stall, his head hanging over the side of the railing, ears perked up and alert.

"Hey there, sweet boy," she said, lovingly smoothing her hand over his muzzle. "Are you ready to get out of here?"

Prairie Prestige whinnied, and MJ couldn't help but smile. Her horse was her "ride or die," and where she went, so did he. Now ten years old, Prairie Prestige had been gelded, stood fifteen hands tall, sported a beautiful bay color and had a white diamond marking between his eyes. He was a beautiful horse by all standards and the only family she had left now. From that first night, when MJ saved his life, and when he lost his mother with Pixie succumbing to the complications of his difficult birth, an unbreakable bond had been formed between them. Like him, MJ's mother had died giving birth to her, so she and Prairie Prestige were orphans and that made them kindred spirits.

Grabbing a lead rope, she opened the gate, patted him on the neck, as she clipped the rope to his halter and led him out of the stall. As if knowing that they were about to escape, he quickly loaded onto the trailer.

"Good boy," she said, closing the tailgate and giving him a pat on the rump. "It's you and me now."

Prairie Prestige snorted in response as she climbed into the cab of the truck and surveyed the farmyard and farmhouse one last time. Closing her eyes, she breathed in deeply, letting out a long, shaky exhale as memories of her wonderful childhood washed over her and an excruciating anguish rose in her chest, threatening to choke her. With bittersweet tears in her eyes and a hard, painful swallow, she pulled the truck out of the driveway, leaving the only home she had ever known in the rear-view mirror.

* * *

IT HAD BEEN APPROXIMATELY eight hours since she left her family farm and had only stopped once to water Prairie at a truck stop just past the Alberta border and take him for a walk along the grassy knoll beyond the parking lot. They were now about an hour west of Saskatoon, Saskatchewan. Knowing she had two 5-gallon containers of water as backup, she pulled into a rest stop where other travelers milled around the washroom and on the grassy area sprinkled with wooden picnic tables. This was as good a place as any to take Prairie out to stretch and to catch a few hours of sleep before she set back onto the road. Parking off to the side, she got out of the cab and reached into the trailer, patting Prairie's neck. "I'll be right back, boy."

She made her way towards the washroom, took care of her needs, and as she washed her hands, she stared a moment at her reflection, the faint brown of a fading bruise still visible on her cheekbone. Chet was going to be furious when he came home to an empty house and even more livid when he figured out that she had left him. *Will he report me missing? Will he try to look for me?* She reached up and touched her dirty blonde hair, the soft waves sliding through her fingers. She had always loved her blonde locks, Chet once calling her his blonde bombshell, but now looking at her hair, it represented the old her, the girl who allowed herself to be controlled and abused. If she was going to be this new brave woman, perhaps a new look was in order. Having already decided to go by Jane in her new life, not only would a new look help her lie low, but it would also help her embrace this new life she was creating for herself. Letting the strands fall from her fingers, she cocked her head to the side. *Perhaps auburn. Like Anne of Green Gables.* She always liked that story. A sassy, smart young orphan going to live with two older siblings on their farm. Not too far a stretch from her actual story. She smiled, *yes, I think auburn would do. In Saskatoon, I'll purchase what I need and dye my hair at the next roadside stop.*

Exiting the washroom, MJ was surprised to see that the sun had faded and twilight was setting in. Glancing around her, the rest stop was eerily quiet with all but one of the vehicles having moved on to their destinations. A large Ford F150 truck parked a short distance from hers, and a man in a cowboy hat was leaning on her trailer, his hand inside reaching for Prairie. The hair on her arms stood on end, and she gulped down, fear rising in her throat as she called out across the lot. "Hey what are you doing?" Approaching cautiously, she unzipped her purse and grabbed her truck keys, lacing them through her fingers like a weapon.

The man stepped away from the trailer, his hands up in the air, and his face became visible in the motion spotlight of the parking lot. Before her stood the epitome of a rugged cowboy. An impossibly handsome man with light brown hair and a dusting of stubble that rimmed his masculine jaw. He was dressed in a dark blue western shirt that showed off a taut physique, and faded Wranglers that stretched over muscular thighs. He removed his well-loved tan-colored Stetson cowboy hat, and his brown eyes skirted over her, gleaming with an amused curiosity.

"Pardon me, Ma'am." he said, his eyes going soft like melting chocolate and reflecting kindness. "I suppose I should have asked."

"I believe that would be common sense." She replied, raising her chin, surprising herself with her boldness and trying not to be affected by his ridiculously handsome face.

"Again, my apologies," he said, slipping a hand into his pocket, putting his hat back on his head and apprehensively glancing back at the trailer. "I hope you don't mind my saying this, but you have a beautiful horse there. Arabian?" he asked. MJ nodded, striding closer to the trailer, her breaths coming out labored and her pulse quick with nervousness. "I thought so. Well, he sure is a beauty. I have Arabians and a few thoroughbreds back home," he said, gesturing over to his truck, the sign on the side saying, Donahue Equine Therapy, Primrose, Manitoba. He stepped forward carefully, coming closer and stretched out his large, calloused hand to her in greeting. "I'm Kolt Donahue."

Hesitating, her eyes flitted to his truck, trying to quickly memorize the phone number there if this encounter went all horror movie on her. With that passing thought, she stuffed her hands into the pockets of her jeans, declining his greeting.

Letting out a low chuckle, Kolt pulled his hand away

and said, "Sorry again, I get it. Strange cowboy at a rest stop. Having grown up in a small town myself, I'm a bit too trusting, I guess. Always thinking the best of people rather than the worst."

Small town. A smile tugged at MJ's lips, but she quickly cleared her throat as she stepped up to her trailer and unlatched the gate.

* * *

What a treat this is? After a long drive from out west, the need to pull over and rest his eyes became abundantly clear about ten miles ago. Familiar with this roadside rest stop, Kolt pulled in, expecting to find a quiet spot in the parking lot where he could tip his hat over his eyes and catch a few winks before he made the remainder of the drive home to Southern Manitoba. What he wasn't expecting to encounter was one of the nicest Arabian horses he had ever seen and its mysterious and stunningly gorgeous owner. From a distance he observed as she entered her trailer, talked to her horse in low soft tones, hooked a lead rope to his halter and backed him out of the trailer.

"How tall is he?" he asked, taking genuine interest in the noble beast with its finely chiseled head and long arching back.

"15 hands," she answered quietly, barely loud enough for him to hear her.

"Wow, he's a tall one," he said, approaching slowly. "Do you mind if I take a good look at him?"

Nodding hesitantly, she stopped under the parking lot

light. He approached, aware of how cautious and apprehensive her gaze was as he rounded the horse and approached him, running his hand over his sloping back and over to his neck, giving the beautiful gelding a scratch.

"What's his name?" He asked, averting his gaze and noticing her shoulders ease slightly as he scratched the horse between the ears.

"Prairie Prestige," she answered, looking up at him shyly, her golden hazel eyes mesmerizing in the stark lamplight. *My god she's pretty.* His eyes were getting lost in her stare for a moment before her gaze drifted to her horse. Kolt smiled, seeing the adoration surrounding the pair, the connection between them evident as her horse nuzzled her cheek with its muzzle. He had seen that kind of connection before, with the clients they worked with. A mutual understanding and trust between humans and beasts. He had that kind of connection with his own horse. But something told him these two were special. Their connection was deeper, and more profound than the usual trust between horse and owner.

Stepping back, not wanting her to put her guard back up, he glanced at the box of her truck, filled to the brim and covered with a tarp, his eyes drifting down to the Alberta license plates. *Is she moving? Is she headed east? Does she have a destination in mind? If I ask, will she answer? Might as well go for it, Donahue.*

"Looks like you're moving there," he commented, his eyes darting to the bed of her truck, then back to her. "I hope you don't mind my asking, but where are you headed?"

Stopping at the edge of the parking lot and letting the lead rope slack for her horse to take long pulls of the grass on the edge, she gave him an untrusting look, then sighed as she answered simply, "I'm not sure yet."

Not sure yet. A thought came to him, and before he could stop himself, he said, "Perhaps settling in the heart of the prairies would suit you."

Her eyes flitted to him, curiosity reflected in her hazel orbs as she asked, "Where would that be?"

"Primrose, Manitoba, a pretty little prairie town, declared the exact center of Canada. It's a quiet, unassuming, and thriving town surrounded by fields and farms. It's honestly an amazing place to live," he said as he leaned against his truck and surveyed her carefully for her reaction.

"Are you the mayor or something?" she asked, a cheeky grin tugging at her lips.

Kolt let out a low chuckle as his smile grew wide, amused by her sarcastic question. He glanced down, randomly kicking a stone with his cowboy boot before meeting her eyes again. "No, but I have lived there my whole life, and I can vouch for our hospitality. Plus, if you are looking for a place to board Prairie Prestige, I know a farmer that may have room." Turning, she met his stare, and seeing he had piqued her interest, he continued. "How about I leave you with a few names and numbers and you can decide for yourself?"

Kolt opened his truck door and reached for a pen and paper from his console. Closing the door, he leaned on his truck and jotted a few numbers down for her. His friends, Ben and Ever Hastings' number at Prairie Sky Acres,

Hayden Hastings at Hastings Hardware, Ms. Lynette, a one stop welcoming committee for Primrose, and lastly his cell phone number. That last number, a bit presumptuous but if there was even a chance he would see this intriguing mystery woman again, he was going to take it. Even better in his small town. Handing her the paper, she looked down at it, her eyes scanning the information, and she glanced up at him, meeting his gaze with softened eyes and a grateful smile as she replied, "Thank you."

He nodded, tipping his hat to her as he said, "You're welcome. Now, I better get some sleep before I get on the road again. I truly hope you consider Primrose. I think you would like it there." With that, he rounded his truck to get in, the weariness of the drive weighing him down. As he reached for the handle of his truck, he doubled back and shouted over to her. "By the way, what's your name?"

The gorgeous mystery woman stopped, her horse nudging her forward as a beautiful smile tugged at her lips, and she replied, "Jane, just call me Jane."

CHAPTER 2

The town sign for Primrose, Manitoba, came into view. A charming sign with bold scrolling letters and a cluster of pink and red roses gracing the corner. MJ smiled, rolling down her truck window and feeling a cool spring breeze feather through her newly dyed auburn hair. This town was as cute and quaint as her roadside cowboy had promised. Making a pass-through town, she took in the whole of main street, with a feed mill at its center and surrounded on either side by businesses like a garage, bank, insurance agency, law office, bakery, diner with gas bar and even a Chinese food restaurant. Immediately, she spotted the Hardware store on Kolt's list, knowing she needed to stop there first after she explored the rest of the town. She found two schools, one primary and one high school, a fire hall, a recreation center, and a library. By the time she was done, she couldn't think of a better place for her and Prairie to settle. Plus, who would think of looking for her in this small town? Surely Chet would never consider it. And that gave her a sense of safety that she desperately needed right now. Pulling up along the side of Hastings Hardware, MJ got out of the cab, ran her hand over the trailer, and reached in to scratch Prairie's neck. He let out a snort in response, making her smile. It had been a long journey for her horse, and although he had been a trooper, MJ was hoping to secure a place for him to stay before she considered her accommodation options.

Entering the hardware store, a petite blonde woman standing behind the counter, with an adorable little girl, all rosy-cheeked and golden blonde that MJ guessed to be approximately three years old, propped up on the counter.

"Hi there!" the woman greeted, picking up the toddler and coming around the counter. "Is there anything I can help you with?"

"Yes, I was hoping to speak to Hayden Hastings." MJ said, her eyes darting around the store.

"Oh, okay! Hayden should be back anytime. He just went to deliver some lumber to a customer. You are welcome to wait here with me and Blakely," the woman said, tickling the little girl, whose bright blue eyes danced with delight as she giggled. MJ smiled, the sound of the toddler's laughter warming her heart. The woman turned her attention back to MJ, and she put out her slender hand. "I don't think I've seen you around here before. I'm Whitney Hastings, Hayden's wife."

"Jane, nice to meet you." MJ said, offering her hand in return. "I was given Hayden's name by Kolt Donahue. He said Hayden would know where I could find a place to stay here in town and said his brother may have room to board my horse."

"Horsey!" the little girl repeated excitedly.

MJ beamed at the cute little girl and nodded.

Just then the chime of the door sounded, and a very handsome dark-haired, blue-eyed man walked in wearing a shirt that said Hastings Hardware. He immediately zeroed in on the little girl and lifted her from her mother's arms, swinging her around and planting kisses on her cherub cheeks. The little girl squealed and giggled as he settled the child on his hip, then leaned in, giving Whitney the most loving look before brushing his lips sweetly to hers. MJ stood there, almost feeling like she should look away; however, the gesture was so lovely; it made her heart swell. *This must be Hayden.* Hayden turned, his piercing blue eyes capturing her as he offered MJ a charming smile. "You must be Jane. Kolt came by yesterday when he got back to town and said you would be dropping by."

He did? That was awfully presumptuous for someone she had just met, and yet she couldn't help but smile internally at his certainty.

"Yes, I am. I was told you were the one to talk to about a place to stay and about where I can board my horse." She said.

Hayden nodded and turned to Whitney, their eyes communicating in silent conversation. Whitney nodded and turned to MJ. "We have a little cottage on our property. We built it for when my parents come into town, but they won't be coming for several months, and if they do, they can stay with us in the main house. We have rented it out a few times with Airbnb, but if you want to stay there, you're more than welcome."

MJ stared at them, taking a moment to slow blink as she absorbed their offer. These people didn't even know her, and they were offering her their cottage? "That is so generous." She stuttered. "I really wouldn't want to put you out or cause you to lose rental income."

Whitney waved her hand in the air, dismissing MJ's concerns. "Seriously, we know it will be hard to find a place quickly, and the Bed and Breakfast on the edge of town is currently closed for renovations. It will give you time to figure out if you want to stay in our little town, and if you do, we can either figure out a rental situation or you can look for another place. The choice is yours. But no rush, seriously, you're not putting us out at all."

"Plus, then you will be close to your horse, as my brother's farm is just two miles away from our property and the cottage." Hayden added, putting his arm around Whitney.

MJ felt overwhelmed with gratitude, swallowing back the emotion that seemed to want to rise to the surface. *These people are so nice.* "Thank you."

"Any friend of Kolt's is a friend of mine." Hayden said with a wink. "Now, let me give you directions to Prairie Sky."

* * *

FOLLOWING the directions Hayden gave her, MJ slowed at the driveway, glancing up at the sign that said Prairie Sky Acres. The farm sign was bright and friendly with its silhouettes of a horse, llama, and sheep. She glanced down at the long driveway, a pretty yellow farmhouse off to the right and in the center of the yard set a little further back was a large, red hip roof barn surrounded by paddocks. *Perfect.*

Turning onto the driveway, a woman stood from where she sat on the front porch and started walking down the stairs towards the walkway. MJ parked and exited the cab, rounding the front of the truck to meet her. The woman was tall, much taller than her, strikingly beautiful with mahogany hair that cascaded down her back in natural waves and soft friendly hazel eyes. Her lips rose in a welcoming smile. "You must be Jane," she said, offering her hand out to her in greeting. "I'm Ever Hastings. Whitney just called me saying you needed boarding for your horse."

Accepting her hand, MJ nodded and replied, "I'm new to town, and Kolt Donahue recommended your farm." MJ glanced around her — the farmyard, pretty and oozing with prairie charm. "Your place is gorgeous."

"Thank you. It's my family's farm. My favorite thing is the view." She said, gesturing to the expansive front lawn with its nicely mowed grass and neighboured by a field on either side. Beyond the front lawn lay one of the most beautiful skies MJ had ever seen. The April day had been crisp and clear, just a cloudless blue sky, but now as dusk was drawing near, bright bands of pink, violet and orange danced across the sky in a gorgeous display.

"It's miraculous." MJ responded with the first word to enter her head.

"Agreed." Ever replied with a contented sigh as they

stood there a moment relishing the view. "Let's go have a seat on the porch while we wait for Ben," she suggested as she gestured for MJ to follow her down the pathway to the porch stairs. "My husband is just upstairs tucking in our son Luke. He is all about his Daddy these days."

MJ smiled, taking in the casual collection of outdoor furniture and the easel, canvas and cart with paint supplies set up in the corner. The beginnings of an exquisite painting on display.

Ever caught her gaze at her unfinished work and smiled. "I'm an artist, a painter mostly, and when the weather turns warmer, I like to paint right here on the porch." She said, gesturing to a wooden rocking chair and taking a seat on a white bench situated against the house under a large picture window.

Like Hayden and Whitney, Ever had a laid-back air about her, making her feel instantly comfortable. Just as MJ took a seat, the storm door opened, and the largest man MJ had ever seen walked out onto the porch. Tall and hulking with big shoulders and arms framing his expansive chest, he had a fully bearded face that was threaded with grey, dark short hair with greying temples and the kindest, gentlest blue eyes that crinkled at the corners. Everything about this man should give her pause, perhaps make her retreat, but she could feel his calming aura as soon as he walked onto the porch, and she couldn't help but feel safe in his presence.

"Hey, sweetheart," he said, settling down next to his wife and resting his large muscular arm on the back of the bench. "That Luke is a tough cookie to crack. He made me read three books before finally agreeing to go to sleep."

Ever let out a knowing laugh and nodded her head as she reached up and threaded her fingers through his beard with affection. "Thank you, babe."

"Anytime," he replied lovingly as his gaze drifted languidly over to MJ.

"This is Jane, the friend of Kolt's that Hayden called you about," Ever said, and he nodded in response.

"Ah yes. Welcome to Prairie Sky," Ben said in a deep, rich baritone as he leaned towards her and put out his large hand in greeting. She accepted it with a firm shake. "I heard you're looking for a place to board your horse. Why don't we go to your trailer and bring him out? Where have you been traveling from?"

"Out west." MJ answered vaguely. "Been on the road a few days, Prairie is antsy to run, I think."

"I bet!" Ever exclaimed, clapping her hands and rising from the bench. "Prairie, you said?"

"Yes, Prairie Prestige." MJ followed her down the stairs, Ben flagging her.

MJ reached the trailer and unlatched the gate. Prairie snorted in greeting as she climbed inside the trailer and ran her hands over his rump and back. His muscles twitched, almost vibrating in response, and she could feel his need to get out of the trailer for more freedom. Ben and Ever stood back and watched patiently. Leaning into his ear, she whispered to him, "What do you think boy, do you want to stay here at Prairie Sky?"

Prairie responded with a whiny, making a smile tug at her lips as she scratched his neck. Replacing the trailer tie with a lead rope to his halter, she backed him out of the trailer and glanced over to Ben and Ever watching with big smiles on their faces. She led him over to the side yard, laxing the lead to let him graze.

"He sure is a beauty." Ben said, admiring Prairie. "Arabian and gelded?"

"Yes," MJ answered, patting Prairie's neck.

"That's good," he said, approaching Prairie slowly and meeting MJ's gaze. "Do you mind if I get acquainted with him?"

MJ's first instinct was to hesitate, but something about this man again made her feel at ease. "Ah, yeah, sure," she replied, handing him the lead rope, and slowly backing away from Ben and Prairie.

A whinny from one of the paddocks caused Prairie's posture to perk up straight, his neck long and ears erect and alert. Ben talked to him in low, calming tones, MJ making out the faint murmurs.

"Do you want to go down there and meet some new friends?" Ben asked, walking forward, keeping the lead rope lax and casual so as not to alarm Prairie.

Ever leaned into MJ and said, "Ben is a bit of a horse whisperer."

MJ grinned and followed as he led Prairie across the yard and over to the paddock where four Arabian horses, two mares and two geldings, stood, curious and alert.

Ben tightened the lead rope slowly, bringing Prairie face to face with the other horses. They snorted and whined as they sniffed and touched muzzles.

"Prairie hasn't socialized much." MJ said, concerned that Ben would simply put him in the pen with the other horses.

"Ben is going to give him an adjoining paddock for a

while, so if Prairie doesn't want to socialize, he doesn't have to. It's the best way to get them used to each other." Ever reassured.

MJ nodded as Ben walked Prairie over to a smaller paddock near the back of the yard, between the other horses and a pen with llamas and sheep. Leading him inside, MJ watched as Ben unclipped the lead rope and Prairie turned his head to her as if asking for approval to let loose. MJ nodded and yelled out, "Go on, boy!"

With that, Prairie took off, circling the paddock, snorting and whinnying, shaking out his mane, all his pent-up energy coming out in a steady gallop. Ben exited the paddock and joined MJ and Ever leaning against the fence.

"Happy as a clam." Ben said, his eyes crinkling with a large grin. "How do you know our resident rodeo star, Kolt Donahue?"

Rodeo star? That was new information. MJ looked up at Ben. "We met at a roadside stop just west of Saskatoon. He told me about Primrose and, well, I didn't have a destination in mind, so here I am."

"Well, we hope you decide to stay because Primrose is definitely a special place to belong. Trust me, I know." Ever said, glancing up at Ben, sharing a knowing look with each other.

They stood there watching Prairie for a while, trotting, and galloping around the pen, stopping where the other horses curiously watched him and leaning into them cautiously. *I think he'll be happy here.* The feeling of uncertainty slowly lifted from her shoulders. Suddenly something occurred to her, and she frowned as disappointment and worry filled her chest. *How am I going to afford to keep Prairie here?* She had limited funds, a lot of the money she saved already gone from the travel expenses alone.

"I...I don't have a lot of money, and I know boarding costs a lot. I don't know how long I'll be able to keep Prairie here." MJ said, glancing over to Prairie, her mouth turning down and heart sinking for her horse.

"Well, I'm sure we can figure something out. I could use some help around here, and if you're willing to help some mornings, I could waive any boarding costs." Ben said, glancing down at her, his eyes kind and understanding. "I could use some help mucking out stalls, doing the morning chores and such. Ever used to help me, but now with the kids, and her busy with commission work, it's just little old me," he said with a wink.

MJ giggled, liking his sense of humor before his offer registered in her mind and emotion rose, causing a constricting lump to form in her throat. "That's so incredibly generous of you both," she managed, looking between both Ben and Ever.

Ever set her hand on MJ's shoulder, the gesture both kind and comforting. "You will find that we here in Primrose are generally kind and generous folks. If we can help someone out, we will." She said with a kind smile.

"Okay, now that we've figured things out, you can start as soon as you're settled, sound good?" Ben asked. MJ nodded. "Now, let me give you a tour of Big Red," he added, gesturing to the large red hip roof barn.

"Then, I'll show you how to get to Hayden and Whitney's, and help you get settled in." Ever said. "You must be exhausted."

* * *

KOLT HAD GOTTEN a call from Hayden five days ago, that "Just Jane" had arrived in Primrose and was now staying in their cottage on their property. Everything about knowing that this intriguing, beautiful and mysterious woman was now in his hometown, only mere miles away from him, made him itch to find her and see her again. Never had he had such a visceral response to a woman before. He met his share of women; in fact, most of the buckle bunnies threw themselves at him on the regular. But that was not his scene. At least not anymore.

At 35, he had found his own success, not only within the rodeo ring but also with his family's equine therapy business. His family farm had become quite lucrative, and he had followed his father's dream and legacy to a tee. Now, as the man of the house, living with his mother and younger sister, he was following through with what his father had started, and for that he was immeasurably proud. He had a rich and fulfilling life, but all that was missing was a love for the ages, like his parents shared, to make his life complete.

He thought about Jane, knowing at first glance that she was much younger than him, his best guess by at least ten years. *Does age matter when it comes to the heart?* His parents had a large age gap. With almost 20 years between them when they got together, their love endured the scrutinizing looks at the ages of 20 and 39, and somehow despite everyone's strong opinions they made it work, enjoying 36 years happily married.

Kolt shook his head at his thoughts, chuckling lightly to himself. *One chance meeting with a beautiful young woman at a roadside stop and I'm planning my forever with her. Slow down, Donahue.* She was intriguing, though, and incredibly beautiful, in a "natural, doesn't realize how stunning she actually is" kind of way. And mysterious too. He remembered how cautious and guarded she was, unsure if his kindness was genuine. How she called herself "Just Jane". Like she had wanted to stay anonymous and hadn't been able to trust people. That thought gave him pause.

She was alone when they met, seemingly with all her worldly belongings in the bed of her truck. No particular destination in mind. *Perhaps she needed a clean slate, or perhaps she was hurt or betrayed in the past.* The thought of that made his gut clench. *Who could hurt such a precious woman?* If he had a woman like her, he would show her what it was like to be cherished and cared for.

"Hey, Kolt!" his sister Georgie said, stepping into the feed room, and putting her hands on her hips with an amused look on her face. "What's got you all distracted, big brother? I tried calling your name like a half a dozen times."

Kolt shrugged, filling the buckets with feed and picking them up. Brushing past his sister, he walked out of the barn as he answered, "Just a lot on my mind."

Georgie followed him, determined to make him talk and pry further. Kolt grumbled under his breath, his annoyance rising. His sister was six years his junior and still took her pesky little sister role very seriously. She watched him empty the buckets into the feeding troughs as the horses came over, digging their muzzles into the feed. He exited the paddock, and as he passed, she asked. "Does this have anything to do with that mystery girl that's staying with Hayden and Whitney?" He stiffened, and her eyes twinkled with delight at his discomfort. "I was talking to Ever yesterday at the bakery, and she said you were the one that "recommended" she come to Primrose," she said, air quoting with a smirk. "Something about a roadside meeting at a rest stop. Kind of serendipitous, don't you think?"

Kolt set the feed buckets back down in the feed room and turned to meet his sister's gaze and with a little chuckle and a shake of his head, he asked, "You love living here, don't you?"

"Of course."

"Then why wouldn't you recommend someone to settle here?" he asked, squinting his eyes.

Georgie let out a little guffaw. "Just saying, Kolt. It was kind of suspicious when Ever told me about her. Apparently, she is young and super pretty. A true, humble and sweet farm girl." Georgie continued shrugging her shoulders. "Kind of sounds perfect for you."

"We'll see." Kolt responded under his breath, looking away, his cheeks flushing a little with his sister's observations.

Georgie set her hand on his shoulder, and he looked up from his work, meeting her gaze. "I just want you to find happiness, like Mom and Dad. You work so hard, Kolt, and you deserve to have a good woman by your side. I, as well as anyone, know how hard it is to find someone around here. And everyone new that comes into town gets snapped up so fast." She says with a frown and a shake of her head. "Finding love is hard in a small town."

He put his hands on his hips and a slow grin curled his lips as he said, "You know, you could call off the search party, Georgie. You could easily have your happily ever after if you would just open up your eyes to what is right in front of you."

Her back stiffened, and her eyes narrowed into slits as she put her hands on her hips in defense. "Please tell me you are not talking about Brooks Isley?"

"Who else?" he asked, flashing her a "see, I can dish it out too" look. "That guy has been crazy about you since you were kids, and you refuse to give him a chance."

"We are just friends. He's my best friend, so I don't think of him that way," she replied with exasperation as he passed her and walked out of the feed room. "Stop changing the subject. What are you going to do about Jane?"

CHAPTER 3

Kolt pulled up to the farmhouse at Prairie Sky Acres next to Jane's truck. Having run into Ben in town, he knew Jane was here alone from their conversation and Ben was okay with him paying her a visit. A flood of anxiousness filled him. The vision of that beautiful face, framed by her long blonde hair and gorgeous hazel eyes, still burned in his brain. Walking into the barn, he glanced around, an old farm cat the only one there to greet him as it rubbed against his jean clad leg. Leaning down, he gave it a scratch and scanned the aisle for any glimpse of the woman he had been thinking about incessantly since they met. Glancing into the office, tack room and feed room, with no sign of her, he approached the side door and that's when he heard her. That soft, sweet voice as she talked to her horse. Approaching the door quietly, he listened.

"How do you like it here, boy?" she asked. "I know it's not home yet, but perhaps it could be."

Kolt's ears perked up, curiosity washing over him as he stayed in the shadows and listened.

"I miss the farm too, all the memories of Grandma and Grandpa," she continued, melancholy in her sweet voice. "But they're nice here in Primrose, don't you think? I think we're safe here too, and that's all that matters."

Kolt pressed his back into the wall, her words echoing in his ear. *We're safe here. Were they in danger?*

"He'll never find us here." She went on. "And he'll never hurt me again or get to you."

Kolt's stomach fell with her words, her initial reaction to him making so much more sense. *Who is she hiding from, and what had he done to her?* He needed to tread lightly with Jane. That was evident.

For a moment he considered leaving, feeling guilty about eavesdropping; however, his desire to see her again was too great. Making the decision to make his presence known, he exclaimed, "Oh, there you are!" as he walked through the barn door and sauntered over to her.

MJ moved around the front of Prairie, ducking under the lead rope with a horse brush in her hand. Untrusting eyes flashed with recognition and enough apprehension to confirm his suspicions, and her change in appearance tracked with what he just overheard. Her once blonde hair, now a stunning deep auburn color. Kolt took a step back, surprised by the change, yet the more he took in the rich color of her hair and how it accentuated the green and flecks of amber in her hazel eyes, he was captivated by how striking she was. With her makeup-free face, lightly freckled skin, high-arched brows, long lashes, and perfectly full lips, she was without question a stunning woman. His eyes roamed unapologetically to her body, her petite frame clad in an old flannel shirt tucked into faded boot-cut jeans that hugged her curves just right and slipped into a pair of dusty, worn brown cowboy boots. Realizing he had been staring, he corrected himself and cleared his throat before his eyes drifted back to hers, a hint of amusement in their depths as he said the first thing that came to his mind, "I like the hair."

Instinctively she touched her locks, running her fingers down a long wavy lock and met his eyes, her hazel orbs softening with the compliment. "Thanks," she said, setting the horse brush down and stuffing her hands in her pockets as she rocked back and forth on her booted feet.

It came across as so endearingly sweet it made Kolt grin as he asked, "How is Prairie Prestige adjusting to his new environment?"

She turned, running her hand over Prairie's mane and scratching between his ears, making him lower his head and lean into her touch. "I think he likes it here. He seems to have taken to the other horses, and Ben and Ever have been so good to him. He seems happy so far."

"Ben and Ever are good people," Kolt said as he approached her and Prairie, running his hand over the slope of Prairie's back. Prairie turned his head, craning his neck and letting out a snort.

Jane rubbed his neck and whispered to him, "It's okay, boy."

It was not lost on Kolt that Jane and Prairie were bound together, their connection evident upon their first meeting, and he smiled. "How are you doing? Are you all settled in at Hayden and Whitney's cottage?"

Cocking an eyebrow at him, she asked, "Are you checking in on me?"

"I might be." he chuckled, turning to face her. "I mean, I did recommend you to my small town, so I need to ensure we're living up to the hype."

Jane met his gaze, her hazel eyes sparkling. "I'm settled in, and so far, so good. The town is not disappointing me. At least the parts of it I have experienced. Mostly, I have just been going from the cottage to the farm every day."

"You mean to tell me you have been in Primrose a whole week and you haven't experienced the greasy goodness from the Eazy?" he said with a laugh as he leaned against the wooden fence and watched her brush through Prairie's mane.

"I haven't had the pleasure." She replied with a little giggle and then crinkled up her nose. "Although with that description, I'm not sure I want to."

"Do you like burgers and homemade fries?" he asked.

"I mean, who doesn't?" she answered, turning to him.

"Then, "Just Jane", would you like to join me for lunch at the Eazy?" he asked, meeting her gaze. Hesitating, she looked away, turning her attention back to Prairie, and stroking his neck with the brush. Apprehension oozed off her as his question hung in the air between them. "Just two horse-loving new friends, sharing a meal," he added, stuffing his hands into his pockets, and staring down at his boots, hoping his break in eye contact would ease her a bit. "I don't even have to pay if you don't want me to, even though that goes against my basic country gentleman nature."

Jane let out a guffaw and turned to him, her hand on her hip. "Oh, you're going to pay," she answered cheekily. "Wouldn't want to force you to stray from your gentlemanly ways, RC."

"RC?" he asked, his lips coming up in a lopsided smirk as he looked to her for an explanation.

With a grin, she replied, "Roadside Cowboy, of course.

* * *

THEY DECIDED to meet at the Eazy, MJ needing to go back to the cottage to shower and clean up. Besides, she needed a moment alone to gather her thoughts. Being around Kolt made her nervous, and she wasn't sure why exactly that was. Perhaps it was his ruggedly handsome face or his old-school gentlemanly charm and quality that was beyond attractive. Maybe it was the sweetness he exuded that she wasn't sure she could trust. Chet had been sweet at first, more than sweet actually. She had considered him the perfect boyfriend until that first bruise. The memory of that day sat like a stone in the pit of her stomach, and she had to breathe in and out slowly to calm her heart that was ready to race.

It had been just over a week since she left her Alberta home and not a message from Chet. He was scheduled to arrive home a few days ago, and surely her absence would have registered by now. Yet, her phone was empty. No texts, no voicemail, just empty. Not that she wanted to be contacted. She was fully ready to block him or change her number, if necessary, but the radio silence was deafening, and when it came to Chet, quiet always felt like the calm before the storm.

Entering the café, all eyes turned to her, the townies, as they called them back home, leaning into each other to whisper as to who she was. She expected it. It was the way small towns worked. Everyone knew everyone, and if they didn't know you, they were sure to find out about you, either by asking or gossiping.

MJ spotted Kolt at the back of the café occupying a booth and made her way over, weaving through tables of onlookers. Kolt eased casually against the back of the vinyl booth, his hat on the seat next to him as she slid in across from him, settling her purse beside her. She had pulled back her newly auburn hair in a ponytail which was still damp from her shower and was dressed in a jean jacket, a simple pink t-shirt and figure-hugging skinny jeans, that showed off her long legs despite her five-foot five-inch height. It was her favorite pair. A memory of Chet telling her to wear them to look sexy when he returned from the fields flashed back, making her suddenly feel self-conscious and uncomfortable and causing her face to flush. Kolt's brows furrowed as he took in her face, suddenly rosy, and reached over the table, resting his hand beside hers. Not on hers but beside. Although they weren't touching, the gesture felt oddly comforting, and she met his eyes with sincere kindness in their depths. Something about the look he gave her made her think he understood her, maybe knew more about her than she was sharing. With knitted brows, she quickly slipped her hand under the table and rested it on her lap in an attempt to get grounded as she asked herself. *Why can't I just sit here enjoying his company rather than making things weird?*

Kolt sat back, his eyes wary with concern, as the waitress came over, greeting them, putting ice water and menus on the table and then rushing off. This little disruption gave MJ a much-needed distraction as she tried to collect herself.

"If you're hungry, I recommend the burger platter," he said, sliding his menu to the side. She opened the menu, perusing the offerings quickly, the usual diner fare, and put down her menu, setting it over his.

"Sounds good to me." she replied, picking up her water and taking a long drink, letting the cold ice water soothe her nerves and calm her again. She glanced over to him, leaning back against the bench, looking laid back, relaxed and sinfully handsome. Before she met Chet, Kolt was exactly the kind of guy she imagined herself with. A family man, sweet, funny. A little bit of an old-fashioned gentleman. A man like her grandfather. *Grandpa.* Just thinking about her late grandfather made her throat constrict painfully. *No, you're not going to make this even weirder by crying,* she chided herself internally as she looked for something, anything to say. "So, you work with horses and your name is Kolt?" she blurted out, internally groaning at her question.

Kolt let out a little laugh, his deep tenor making her heart inadvertently flip-flop. "Weird, right?" he asked, picking up his ice water. "I have pretty much heard jokes about my name my whole life. But it's a family name, so I'm proud of it." he said with another chuckle. "You're looking at the one and only, Koltson Patrick Donahue. Koltson was my mother's maiden name."

Koltson, she repeated in her head as she traced her fingertip through the condensation on her glass and smiled up at him, answering, "I like it."

Kolt leaned on his elbows, his surveying eyes on her but not in an uncomfortable way. She knew the question was coming, and she had her answer rehearsed. "So, Just Jane, what's the story behind that? I mean, you must have a last name, middle name, nickname, pen name, alias name…" She sensed he was joking, but his observation hit a little too close to home.

"I prefer to be just Jane," she replied.

"So, like Cher, Madonna, Adele or Bjork?" he asked playfully, emphasizing the K.

MJ couldn't help but giggle as she volleyed, "More like Reba."

"Ah, so you're a country girl through and through then." He replied, nodding his head in approval as he leaned back against the booth, and raised his glass of ice water to his mouth, adding. "That explains the red hair then."

Another giggle escaped her throat; her cheeks hurt from how wide her smile was. Kolt was funny, and she liked this silly side of him that he was revealing to her. It made her feel at ease around him.

"Well then, I like it!" he exclaimed. "The hair, the name, all of it! Nice, simple and practical. Jane it is!"

Their food came, and they talked lightly, the conversation never venturing past her comfort zone, which she appreciated. Mostly they talked about Prairie Prestige, and he shared about his rodeo career. MJ was fascinated to find out that he competed regularly in steer wrestling, tie down roping and team roping. Her grandparents had taken her to the Calgary Stampede when she was fourteen, and she marveled at the power and skill it took to compete in those events. The excitement of the crowd was contagious, and she remembered loving every minute of it.

"Have you ever considered showing Prairie Prestige? You know competing at horse shows?" he asked, popping his last fry into his mouth, and pushing aside his plate. "A horse like that is sure to rank high when competing. It would take some training, but I think he would be amazing."

Truth was, MJ knew a lot about horse shows, having competed with Prairie many times in her teens. It wasn't until her grandparents passed away that she stopped.

"Prairie has shown before." She replied simply, swirling a french fry through a dollop of ketchup on her plate. "It's been about four years since I've shown him, though."

"Oh, so you're familiar with how these shows work. Is this something you want to do again?" Kolt asked with genuine curiosity.

MJ thought about it for a moment. The fond memories of the costumes, excitement of competing and the pride on her grandparents' faces when she came away with a brightly colored ribbon or fancy trophy. She had a box of her winnings back home in the attic, now wishing she had brought them with her. Sadness overwhelmed her, combined with the memory of her loved ones lost, as she answered vaguely, "I am not sure if I want to."

CHAPTER 4

*K*olt lay in bed thinking about his conversation with Jane. She was jumpy during lunch. Whenever the chime of the door sounded, her eyes would dart to the door. She was scared of something, or perhaps someone — of that he was certain. *What or who is she hiding from?* These thoughts had been needling him all day. The sudden hair change, the name he was sure was an alias of sorts, and not sharing exactly where she was from. Everything adding to her mystery and his curiosity was in overdrive. Rolling onto his back, he sighed, staring up at the ceiling, with a million thoughts swirling in his head and knowing tonight was going to be a sleepless night.

"Well, there he is." Emmaline Donahue said as her son came down the staircase and into the kitchen looking exhausted and a little disheveled. Kolt took a seat at the kitchen table, running his hand through his mussed hair. Reaching into the cupboard, she pulled out a mug and poured him a cup of coffee, fixed it the way he liked and set it down next to him. "What's got you overthinking, sweetheart?" she asked, taking a seat across from him, her brows furrowed in worry. "Does it have anything to do with the young woman who's new to Primrose?"

He looked up, meeting her eyes and instantly knowing his mother was privy to the town gossip already. "Let me guess, the gossip mill has been brewing about Jane and I having lunch together yesterday?"

"Her name is Jane, okay and yes, you know how it is, Kolt. I know you don't like it, but you're kind of an elusive bachelor around here, so when you're seen with someone, especially a lovely young woman, the word gets around quickly."

Kolt chuckled, his laugh turning quickly into a deep yawn.

"What's it about her that's getting you all worked up?" his mother asked as she brought her coffee cup to her lips and gingerly took a sip of the hot liquid.

"I don't know exactly, Mom, but it seems like she's been through something, and I can't quite figure it out," he said, meeting his mother's inquiring gaze. "She's jumpy, untrusting, and I think she's hiding here in Primrose from something or someone."

His mother's brows knit together, and she leaned forward, her elbows on the table and hands cradling her coffee cup as she asked, "What makes you say that?"

"I sort of stumbled upon her having a conversation with her horse yesterday when I went to Prairie Sky, and I may have heard a little more than I should have," he confessed guiltily.

A smile tugged at his mother's lips as she asked for

clarification, "She talks to her horse?" He nodded. "Sounds like someone I know," she added, nudging his foot under the table with a grin.

Kolt mirrored her amusement, thinking about all the times he and his rodeo horse, Stetson, had been caught in conversations of their own.

"Jane is different from other girls I've met. She's special. I like her, and I feel this overwhelmingly strong need to help her, and…" he started running his hand over the scruff on his chin. "…protect her from whatever this is that she's running from."

His mother reached out and put her hand on his forearm. "You, Kolt, are a good man. You're a protector, and you've always been someone that wants to help others solve their problems. I am so proud that I raised such a sweet and kind son. If you like this woman and she has or is currently going through something difficult, maybe you just need to take things slow and build a friendship first, grow the trust between you two before you pursue her romantically."

Knowing his mother was right, he nodded. He needed to approach Jane with care, and even if he wanted to jump in feet first, he knew it was going to take some time for her to fully trust that he had good intentions.

Their eyes turned to the front picture window, overlooking the stable and the paddocks, horses dappled through the open pasture expanse.

"Perhaps she needs a little equine therapy to open up," his mother suggested.

Kolt considered her suggestion, his eyes widening as a plan instantly formed in his head. Prairie Prestige was

Jane's entire world, her horse like an extension of herself. When she talked about her horse, her eyes lit up the same way his did when he talked about Stetson. A barrage of ideas threaded through his thoughts. If Jane was going to trust him, he needed to lean into their mutual interest, starting on horseback.

A LOUD RAP at the door of the cottage stirred MJ from her afternoon nap. She had been up early, heading to Prairie Sky to do the morning chores and after a day of farm work that included going for a ride down the road with Prairie, she came home in the early afternoon tired but happy. Once she showered, she slipped her pajamas back on and crawled under the comforter, letting the faint hum of the ceiling fan lull her to sleep.

Slipping out of bed, she padded to the door, wishing there was a peephole so she could vet any visitors. Instead, she cautiously opened the door a crack to find Hayden and Whitney's ten-year-old son, Bauer, standing at her door, his piercing blue eyes sparkling with mischief.

"Hello," she said, opening the door a little more.

"Hi, Miss Jane. Mom wanted to know if you wanted to join us for dinner. Dad is building a fire, and we're going to roast hot dogs and make s'mores." he said excitedly.

Dinner with the Hastings. Jane had all but kept to herself in the three weeks that she had been in Primrose, Hayden and Whitney giving her space as she settled in. They had been kind and checked in on her a few times, but mostly left her to her own devices with the space they had offered her completely self-contained.

"Sure," she replied, smiling down at the cute little boy. "Tell them I will be at the house in 20 minutes."

Bauer flashed her a smile as he spun on his heel and sprinted down the path he came, disappearing through the back patio doors of the main house.

Dressing quickly in a pair of jeans and a sweatshirt, the early May air a little chilly later in the day, she brushed her long mane of auburn hair that was now in askew rebellious curls from falling asleep with wet hair and she took in her reflection as she smoothed her sweaty palms down the front of her jeans.

Why am I so nervous? The truth was, she hadn't done much socializing over the past couple of years. Popular in high school, MJ was always surrounded by friends, but once they graduated, many of her friends moved on to start their own lives, going off to college or university, leaving their small town behind. Although at the time, she wondered if Chet would do the same; he seemed content to stay, so he was all she had left once her friends had dispersed. Looking back, she always thought their lack of outside friends was what bonded them, but now, removed from his control, she realized that he played a hand in her diminishing social circle. In retrospect, she was sure he was trying to isolate her, and her grandparent's death was advantageous for him as once they were gone, she had only him to rely on. *It's amazing the clarity you have when you're no longer in the thick of it.*

Making her way down the path leading to the house,

she saw Hayden coming around the side of the house, his arms full of firewood.

"Hey, Jane! Glad you could join us. Whitney is just in the kitchen, so you can go on inside if you want," he said, pointing his chin towards the house.

MJ nodded in return and did as he suggested, rapping lightly on the patio door. The door slid open, and she was greeted by four pairs of eyes staring up at her with smiling faces. The Hastings kids.

"Let Miss Jane come into the house, for goodness' sake." Whitney said with a laugh, shooing off her brood. The three boys ran back through the patio door giggling, Bauer carrying a soccer ball, leaving only Blakely still peering up at her. Silently, the little girl put her arms out, asking MJ to pick her up.

MJ complied and scooped up the little girl, who was smiling at her shyly. She had always loved kids and did some babysitting when she was a teen, always imagining that one day she would have a bunch of her own. Whitney turned and watched as Jane took a seat at the island and rested Blakely on her knee facing her. Taking her chubby little hand in hers, she traced circles on her palm and sang, "Round and round the garden, like a teddy bear. One step, two step, tickle you under there!" With that, she tickled Blakely's underarm, making her squirm and squeal with delight.

"You're good with her." Whitney commented casually, leaning onto the island. "Do you have any brothers or sisters?"

"No, just me," MJ replied, singing it again at the request of Blakely.

"No one back home wondering where you are then?" Whitney asked.

"No, my grandparents passed away four years ago, and they raised me." MJ revealed, so distracted by the giggling toddler in her lap. "My mother died when I was born."

Whitney's brows furrowed with her answer as she commented. "It must have been lonely on your own."

"Sometimes. But I had Prairie and the farm and…" she stopped, suddenly realizing how much she was divulging and cleared her throat. "I was fine."

Whitney gave her a gentle smile, picked up a serrated bread knife and cut hotdog buns, then set them into a bowl. "I hope you like hotdogs and s'mores because my crew has been looking forward to this all day. Can you grab that bowl of chips?"

MJ watched as Whitney exited through the patio door, little Blakely climbing off her lap and following her mother as MJ internally chided herself. *You're going to have to be careful about what you share. Sharing too much is going to blow your cover.* Yet something told her she could trust the Hastings. Whitney, in particular. In her interactions with Whitney, she came across as knowing that MJ had been through something, and she could relate. It was a hard observation to describe, but she simply knew they had something profound in common and that she was safe staying here with their family.

Exiting the kitchen onto the concrete patio, the three Hastings boys, Bauer, Beckett and Bodhi were kicking around their soccer ball while Blakely was curled up on Hayden's lap as he roasted a hotdog on the end of a stick for her over the fire.

"Come and get your sticks, boys." Whitney yelled as all three boys ran towards her, grabbing their sticks, already pierced with hotdogs, with Whitney telling them to be careful and not poke each other's eyes out.

MJ took a seat across from Hayden and watched the boys trying to carefully roast their hotdogs, while Whitney walked over to Hayden and leaned down, planting an affectionate kiss on his lips. MJ smiled at the scene. *This is family.* Something at one point she had hoped for. Creating a family of her own. That thought suddenly made her sad, emotion welling up in her chest. Taking a deep breath in, trying to steady herself, she stood from her lawn chair ready to excuse herself, feigning sickness so she could flee back to the little cottage, but Whitney approached her, handing her a stick with a hotdog already speared.

"Here you go," Whitney said, her gentle eyes meeting hers, something unspoken passing between them. "There are buns and all the fixings you need on the picnic table, okay?" MJ nodded, swallowing down the lump that had been forming in her throat and let out a sharp exhale. Whitney put her hand on her shoulder. "Just help yourself and make yourself at home."

MJ eased, choosing to stay and after a casual dinner complete with fire-kissed s'mores and lots of laughter compliments of the kids, she felt lighter. The sun was going down, and Hayden offered to get the kids washed up and tucked into bed, leaving MJ and Whitney sitting quietly by the fire. Silence fell on the pair as they watched the flames lick the air and the wood crackle as it burned. Just sitting here like this was soothing, and MJ couldn't remember a time she had felt this content, carefree and relaxed.

"What is it about a bonfire that is so calming?" Whitney asked with a contented sigh. "You know, sometimes I like to just sit out here quietly by the fire and reflect on my life." MJ turned her head towards Whitney, the glow of the fire dancing across her face as she stared into the flames. "Hayden and I have been married 11 years, and never did I think this native Torontonian would live outside a small Manitoba town, with a gorgeous husband and four kids." She shook her head and let out a little laugh, her chuckle almost wistful as she continued. "20 years ago, I never would have thought such happiness was possible for me. I was young, stuck in an abusive marriage and honestly didn't know how to get out of the situation. It was a volatile and scary place to be. Those were some dark years."

MJ gulped, feeling Whitney's words, like a confessional, an echo of her life with Chet. Questions started popping into her head. *How did you get out? How did you find the courage to start over?* There were so many questions she wanted to ask. But the only question that felt safe at that moment was simple. "Where is your ex now?"

"Jail," Whitney answered matter-of-factly. "He's eligible for parole in 4 years, I believe."

"Are you scared he'll come find you?" MJ asked, surprised by her own bold questioning.

"Sometimes I mean, I think when you've been abused either physically, mentally, or emotionally, that never completely leaves you. Little things will come out from time to time, reminders of the past that trigger that fear," she said, meeting MJ's gaze and offering her a reassuring smile. "It helps to have good friends and to have the love of someone who accepts you, past and all. Hayden never saw my past as a burden or something to fix. He just loved me as I was, supported me through it and showed me that I could have a second chance at the life and love I always dreamed of."

MJ turned back to the fire, letting those words absorb into her consciousness and wishing she could find that too. *Kolt.* His name popped into her head, and she felt the blush rise to her cheeks. He made her nervous. Her insides turned to jelly when he locked her with his soft, melting chocolate stare. Like she was a book he was dying to read and savor every word from. No man had ever come close to looking at her that way.

"You don't need to tell me your story if you don't want to. But just know, I'm here if you need to talk," Whitney said, reaching over and touching her forearm gently.

MJ's mouth opened, a protest wanting to escape as she looked down at Whitney's comforting hand touching her arm. Lies on the tip of her tongue were ready to be spewed that Whitney had read her wrong, but instead she closed her mouth and gave her a nod in acknowledgement.

The patio door opened, breaking them from their private conversation, and Hayden walked out with a beer in one hand, two wine glasses in the other and a bottle of wine tucked under his arm. "Kids are finally asleep," he said, carefully setting everything down on the picnic table. "Would you ladies like a glass of wine?"

"Yes, please." Whitney replied, turning to MJ. "Would you like a glass?"

MJ smiled, the weight of her secrets feeling a bit lighter from their conversation. "Yes, thank you, Hayden."

That night, for the first time since she had arrived in Primrose, she slept through the night, thoughts of Kolt as her nightlight keeping the monsters of her old life caged in the shadows.

CHAPTER 5

Kolt spotted Jane's truck immediately as he passed Hastings Hardware. Turning his truck around, he made a loop in the feed mill parking lot and doubled back, parking next to her truck. Climbing out of the cab, he made his way to the door, holding it open for a couple exiting and tipping his hat to them. As he walked in, he spotted Jane stocking a display with paintbrushes, dressed in tight blue jeans and a Hastings Hardware T-shirt, her long wavy hair pulled up in a casual ponytail cascading past her shoulder blades.

Approaching her, she was so engrossed in what she was doing that she didn't turn. "Excuse me, Ma'am, what kind of paintbrush would you recommend for painting the side of a barn?

Startled, Jane turned and almost knocked down the entire display as she held her hand to her chest, her chest heaving as if she had just run a race. Her brows furrowing and a flash of actual fear shadowed in her eyes. Kolt immediately felt terrible for frightening her.

"I'm so sorry, Jane, I didn't mean to scare you," he apologized, as he gently touched her arm.

She shook her head, her auburn ponytail wagging as she steadied her breathing. "It's okay Kolt, sorry, I..."

"No need to explain. I shouldn't have snuck up on you," he said, meeting her gaze with regret. "I saw your truck parked outside and thought I would pop in and say, " Hi."

Her eyes met his shyly, her face flushed a pretty pink, and a glimmer of a smile tugged at her beautiful lips as she replied, "Hi."

"Are you working here now?" he asked, as she knelt to pick up the paintbrushes that had fallen to the ground and he crouched down to help her.

"Yeah, a few shifts a week." She replied. "I can't partake in charity forever, and Hayden needed another part-time employee, so we made an arrangement."

"I guess that means that you are staying then." Kolt said, his gaze meeting hers and getting lost a moment in her gorgeous hazel eyes.

Rising to her feet, she cleared her throat and walked over to the counter as she answered with nervousness in her tone, "Primrose is treating Prairie and me well, so no need to move on just yet."

Although her answer wasn't definitive, Kolt loved hearing that. Part of him wondered if he would wake up one day and she would be gone. Just a mirage or figment of his imagination that he conjured up from his dreams. But she was here, slowly incorporating herself into their small town and finding her place within.

"Speaking of Prairie, I was wondering if you wanted to go riding with me sometime?"

"When?" she quickly asked, her eyes darting to meet his, with piqued interest.

"When is your next day off?"

"Tomorrow."

"Why don't you trailer Prairie and come down to my family farm? I would love to show you the business, and we have some amazing trails we can ride down," he replied. "Could I text you, directions?"

"Is this your way of asking me for my phone number?" She asked, cocking an eyebrow at him and giving him what could be considered a flirtatious look.

Smiling, he took the open invitation and leaned on the counter, locking her with an intense stare as he answered, "Perhaps it is. If you haven't already figured it out yet, Just Jane, I kind of like you."

Sweet, endearing rosiness bloomed on the apples of her cheeks as a smile tugged on her lips and she reached into her pocket, pulling out her phone and replied, "Well, in that case."

STOPPING AT THE DRIVEWAY, MJ took in a large sign that said, "Donahue Equine Therapy", and turned down the tree-lined driveway, a large two-story farmhouse coming into view with a full wrap-around porch. Beyond the house stood a tall white barn with what looked to be an arena attached to the back. There was a machine shed off to the side, with a big green John Deere tractor parked inside and a horse trailer beside it as well as a truck top camper. A couple of cars were parked in front of the barn, and to the side of the house was a series of paddocks with around a dozen horses grazing on the long field grass. The warmth of the spring sun glistened off their coats against a blue sky sprinkled with fluffy marshmallow clouds as the backdrop. The farm was pretty and welcoming, and MJ couldn't help but smile, taking it all in.

Parking next to the other vehicles, she got out of her truck and entered the open door of the barn, hearing voices and the laughter of a child inside. A barn kitten scurried past, and MJ dodged it as she ventured deeper into the barn. A beautiful grey Arabian horse was tied up to the door of a box stall as a young boy in a wheelchair was brushing it and talking to a woman dressed in riding crops and a t-shirt that said Donahue Equine Therapy. The woman spotted MJ and leaned into the boy to tell him something before she walked over to greet her. She smiled, her eyes a warm chocolate brown exactly like Kolt's.

"You must be Jane. I'm Kolt's sister, Georgette," she said with a friendly smile. "But please call me Georgie. Kolt's in the arena." She gestured for her to go ahead.

As Jane approached the arena, she could hear the grunt of the horse and the pounding of hooves as Kolt came into view on his horse. Riding a chestnut Quarter Horse, tall, muscular, and strong — he was taking his horse through a series of drills, starting, stopping, getting him to back up, taking his cues with precision. MJ leaned against the cased opening watching, mesmerized by the way he maneuvered his horse all the while, looking like the sexiest cowboy she had ever seen. *Dear Lord, he's handsome.* Ever since he told her he liked her yesterday at the hardware store, her mind was filled with thoughts of Kolt. She liked him too. A lot if she was being honest with herself, even though her mind kept putting up caution signs telling her to keep him at arm's length, reasoning her tumultuous past love life was to blame for her apprehension with Kolt. After her conversation with Whitney around the fire and his admission the day before, something made her want to open up to him. Her gut told her she should try to trust him. So here she was, a decision made that she was going to take it slow and see where things went with Kolt. Allow herself to explore this obvious attraction they seemed to have. *What if Kolt is my second chance, just like Hayden was for Whitney? Would it be fair to deny myself that possibility?* Those types of questions were why she was here. Kolt felt like a new start for her even if she was proceeding cautiously.

Kolt slowed down his horse, leaning forward and patting its neck as his eyes caught on her and she raised her hand in a little wave. With that, his lips curved into a slow smile that did some crazy flip-flop to her heart. *Dear Lord in heaven, I am in so much trouble.*

Kolt rode over and dismounted his horse, rounding him, the leather reigns in his hands. The Quarter Horse snorted and ground its teeth against the metal bit, foam at the corners of its mouth, obviously having been worked hard in the ring. MJ met Kolt's gaze and gestured to his horse, asking permission to approach him.

"This is Stetson," Kolt said. "Stetson, as you could see, is my rodeo horse."

She nodded, admiring the size and strength of his horse, her eyes flitting back to Kolt as she said, "You and Stetson have some pretty slick moves there, RC." Slowly sliding her hand over Stetson's muzzle to scratch him between the ears and he leaned into her touch.

"He's just a big old softie most of the time, but when it comes to rodeo, he's all business." Kolt said with a grin. "I actually have a local rodeo in two weeks, if you want to see Stetson do his thing."

"Just Stetson, not you?" Jane asked, cocking an eyebrow at him. The flirtatious nature of her comment made his pulse quicken. Up until now, Jane had been an anomaly to him. Seemingly unfazed by his flirtations, her guard was so high he was unable to climb over it. It seems he had broken through, and she was starting to show interest in him too. Despite this, he was resolute that he was going to take this as slowly as she needed and follow her lead.

"Mostly for me," he replied honestly as he met her gaze. "I would really love to see you in the crowd, Jane."

Turning, she reached for his hand and replied, "Then I'll be there."

Her touch sent trickles of sensation through his body and straight to his heart. They lingered like that for a moment, her hand grasping his, something so simple feeling nice, natural and oh so right. "I think I should get Prairie out of the trailer and get him saddled up." She said quietly on a breath, looking up at him through her long lashes.

Kolt made no move to let go, not wanting this sweet, simple moment of connection between them to end until Stetson let out a whinny, breaking their revelry and making them both laugh lightly. "C'mon, let's get Prairie. I've got a special place I want to show you."

WITH STETSON and Prairie both saddled and eager, Kolt and MJ set out down the long driveway, turning down the gravel road leading to their farm. Where the Donahue Farm was located, there was more bush than around Prairie Sky Acres, which only had a smattering of trees and was mostly open, surrounded by farmers' fields. Kolt led her down the slope of a ditch to a trail that wound between trees, giving you the illusion that you were getting lost deep in the woods. The trail was well manicured, having obviously been ridden through countless times.

"Are you good?" Kolt asked, glancing behind him as he led the way.

"I am, but where are you taking me?" MJ asked curiously.

"We're almost there. It's just up the trail a bit," he replied.

The trail continued to twist through the trees until a large, expansive clearing revealed itself. A meadow of long prairie grass and the beginnings of colorful wildflowers stood before them untouched and perfect in its simplicity. *This is beautiful.*

Riding up beside Kolt, he noticed her awed expression and suggested, "How about we let the horses graze here a while?"

MJ nodded as he dismounted his horse, and she followed by letting go of Prairie's reins knowing he would stay close to her. Kolt did the same with Stetson, the trust between him and his horse as evident as hers with Prairie.

Leading her over to a large oak tree that shadowed a corner of the meadow with its labyrinth of twisted branches and sprigs of new spring leaves, he lowered himself to the ground, and she sat down beside him in the tall grass. They sat there quietly, taking in the beauty of the warm spring day, but her mind was anything but quiet. The awareness of his proximity next to her was making her mind reel and doing inexplicable things to her body. Everything about Kolt was masculine and strong. He was unquestionably all male by the way he wore his tight Wranglers and filled out a t-shirt, but what made him the sexiest was his gentlemanly nature. He was so gentle, sweet and had a soft kindness in his eyes that felt like a throwback from an old western to a true "oh shucks, howdy ma'am" kind of cowboy and it made butterflies take flight in her belly.

"So, you see that tree line right over there," he said, leaning his head closer to hers as he pointed towards a row of trees with a field beyond them. She nodded. "If we were to ride through the trees on the other side of this clearing, it would lead to 20 acres of farmland. I own everything from the ditch that we crossed to the end of those 20 acres."

She nodded with a smile as he continued, "I feel like this meadow would be a perfect place for a farmyard."

MJ looked around the expansive open space, and she could visualize it as she said, "I can see you building a farmhouse there." She said, pointing to one side of the clearing with close access to the gravel road. "And over there you could build a barn and machine shed. Just leave plenty of space for paddocks. The field beyond could be pastureland unless you want to farm it. Perhaps a combination of alfalfa and orchard grass so you have fodder for the horses through the winter."

Turning her head, she met Kolt's gaze, which flashed with approval, and his lips turned up in a slow grin.

An emerging blush rose to her cheeks, and she looked away. "Sorry, I can see it clearly, I guess."

Kolt put out his hand, palm up and fingers spread. Her eyes flitted down to his large hand, open and inviting, and slowly she placed her hand inside his. His fingers wrapped over hers as the tender warmth of his hand enveloped her, feeling like a hug. "I like your ideas; I've been kind of lost as to what to do here, to be honest. My Dad had our land subdivided years ago and gifted me this parcel on my 25th birthday. I think he wanted us kids to stay close. Georgie has her own parcel of land as well." His eyes drifted over to hers, so much sincerity in their depths. "Not sure what has stopped me from making plans. Perhaps I was hoping to share it with someone special."

Her heart fluttered with his words; this man was so

much deeper than she thought. Kolt wanted to share his life with someone . A partner, an equal. All the things the young hopeless romantic in her hoped to share with Chet at one time. She let out a long, shaky breath, an unexpected emotion rising to the surface with her thoughts. So many hopes and dreams pinned to a man who didn't value her. A man who said what she wanted to hear, telling her that he loved her. A man who hurt her and left deep cavernous scars both inside and out.

"Are you okay?" Kolt asked, giving her hand a squeeze, his soft brown eyes filled with trepidation.

"I will be," she answered simply, looking down at their joined hands. "My life hasn't exactly gone as planned."

"Is that why you and Prairie are here in Primrose?" he asked carefully.

MJ nodded and looked up, meeting his gentle stare, feeling a deep connection radiate between them as she whispered, "It feels safe here with you."

The corners of Kolt's lips curved up, but his eyes remained concerned. "You don't have to tell me what you've been through, Jane, but know I'm never going to hurt you." Kolt said as he reached over and delicately brushed the loose hair from her face, letting his fingertips trace the line of her cheek so gently I made goosebumps form on her skin. "Not here..." he started caressing her face. "And not here." he finished, resting his palm over her heart.

* * *

KOLT WAS sure he had never felt this completely connected to a woman. The man in him wanted to hold her, protect her, and tell her that everything would be okay. Erase all the demons that haunted her and be her shield. But the truth was, he didn't know if it would be. Unless he knew exactly what she had been through and what she was facing, he couldn't make her that promise. But what he could do right now was reassure her that he would do anything in his power to keep her safe if she would let him. Now, here with his hand over her heart, the steady thrum against his palm, all he could think about was how lucky he was to be here with her. That she was letting him in, even a little.

Jane's hand came over his, pressing his palm tighter against her chest, feeling the pounding rhythm grow faster, wilder under his palm. The moment felt intimate. Like one between two lovers. As if they were the earth and moon held together by a gravitational force. *Should I kiss her? Should I make that move? Would she see it as too much too soon? Does she feel the same intense pull that I do?*

All his questions were answered as Jane's hand came up, tracing the stubble along his jaw, and she looked deep into his eyes, her hazel orbs so golden in the midday light as she whispered, "Please kiss me, Kolt."

Slowly, he took off his cowboy hat, trying to steady his rapidly beating heart as he lowered his lips to hers. That first touch of her supple soft lips, so much sweeter than he imagined. As they kissed, he felt her entire body exhale, passing on her fears to him, letting him carry the weight for a while. Their mouths moved together, his hand slipping to her waist, pulling her closer, yet very aware not to push her boundaries. The kiss was tender, not rushed, but savored. Every part of his being awakened with emotion, desire, and the most exquisite tingling sensation. Never in his life had a kiss felt so right, so perfect. Pulling away, Jane slowly opened her eyes, her cheeks flushed and her eyes hazy as if waking from a dream. She smiled, laced her fingers with his and turned, resting her head on his shoulder as she let out a contented sigh. They stayed like that a long time, watching Stetson and Prairie graze on the tall grass as they relished the cool of the shade of the oak tree and watched as thunderheads rumbled far in the distance, promising a spring storm. Yet not even a spring storm matched the storm of emotions burgeoning within his heart.

CHAPTER 6

$\mathcal{P}$ulling into Prairie Sky early the next morning, MJ was still riding high on the bliss of her day with Kolt. After their trail ride, Kolt's mother invited her in for dinner, and she enjoyed a delicious meal, along with interesting conversation and so much laughter her sides still hurt. His mother and sister were so welcoming, and although it was probably far too soon to think this way, she felt a part of his family.

She grinned, feeling the heat rise to her cheeks as she thought about their kiss under the oak tree and how she so boldly initiated it. Kolt was a gentleman with a capital G, and she was sure he wouldn't try to kiss her unless she asked. And boy, that kiss did not disappoint. Never had she been kissed like that before, so tenderly, so gently, everything about it so saccharine sweet and yet with a tempered desire at its core. She had kissed a few boys in her time before Chet came along, and not even one, including Chet, could match that kiss with Kolt.

Instantly her mind drifted to other ways he could use

his lips, and her core pulsed. *Don't go there, MJ.* Sex had never been something that she found satisfying; in fact, she would go so far as to say she didn't like it. Kissing, foreplay, yes; the actual act, no. Chet had been her first, and although she would say the beginning of their relationship had glimpses of passion, it certainly never ignited into a full-blown fire. At least not for her. He was always taking and never giving. Chet was rough. Even when she made it clear, she didn't want to. She shook her head, trying to dispel the harsh memories with Kolt's words repeating in her head. *I am never going to hurt you.* She clutched her heart and could almost feel the warmth of his hand lingering there.

A knock on the driver's side window broke her from her thoughts, and she turned to see Ever's smiling face as she waved at her. Her cheeks stoked into an inferno of embarrassment at being caught daydreaming about Kolt as she opened her door. Ever stepped back for her to slide out of her truck, and she sheepishly glanced up at Ever's amused face.

"I was wondering if you wanted to come inside for a quick breakfast before you and Ben start the morning chores?" She asked with a twinkle in her eye. "But when you didn't get out of your truck, I…"

"Yeah, sorry, I was…" MJ started.

Ever held up her hand, stopping her. "No need to explain. I think I know who you were thinking about," she said with a wink. "Ben called Kolt last night asking about his upcoming rodeo, and he may have mentioned you two went riding. It's no secret to us all that Kolt Donahue is sweet on you, Jane."

MJ blushed even more at this as Ever put her arm around her, leading her down the walkway to the porch. "C'mon inside and enjoy a big farm breakfast while you tell me all about your day with Primrose's resident cowboy."

KOLT CLIMBED INTO THE SHOWER. A long day on horseback made him ache in places his body usually didn't ache. He was starting to feel his age, even though he knew he could have at least ten more years of rodeo if he chose to continue that long. As a roper, his rodeo cowboy lifespan likely would go well into his 40s, but lately, he was wondering why he was continuing with it. Sure, he loved the cheer of the crowd, the challenge of beating his time, and the accolades and money were nice too, but was it worth it? With each rodeo and all the work that went into it, he couldn't help but think if he walked away tomorrow, would he miss it?

Letting the hot water run over his back, he leaned forward, bracing himself against the opposite side of the shower wall, his arms strained as he let the heat of the water soothe his tired muscles. The steam rose around him as his mind drifted to Jane. Yesterday was so much more than he had expected. Although he had no expectations going into the day, the fact that Jane had opened, even a little, made him understand her even better. Someone had hurt her. To what extent he didn't know, but the fact that she was starting to trust him made him confident that she would eventually trust him enough to let him in fully. Every time he thought of her being hurt, mentally, emotionally, physically, his chest would tighten, and his fists would clench. The thought, too much to fathom.

Flashbacks of her face when he told her he would never hurt her floated through his consciousness. Her soft hazel eyes morphed from troubled to trusting. And when she so unexpectedly requested a kiss, he knew he had her permission to pursue her. Something inexplicable happened at that moment. A deep unconscious awareness that he had staked his claim on her, and she had staked her claim on him. What that looked like in the future he wasn't sure yet, but right now, he was going to simply take what she was willing to give, show her the way she deserved to be treated and use every moment he had to make her feel wanted and special. With all of that, if Jane was ever comfortable enough to give herself fully to him, she would know how much it truly meant to him.

Imagining that possibility, being with Jane, body and soul, made an arousal pulse through him. Like an electrical current running from the top of his head to the tips of his toes. The kiss they shared may have been soft, sweet, and restrained, but there was a passion at its edges that told him that the desire he was feeling for her was more than mutual. Their attraction, palpable. *I need to see her again.*

Turning off the shower, Kolt reached for a towel and quickly dried himself. Wrapping the towel around his waist, he opened the door, walking across the hall towards his bedroom. Closing his bedroom door, he took a seat on the side of his bed and reached for his phone.

Swiping it open, a text notification popped up and he smiled. *Jane.* Eagerly he clicked on her text:

Just Jane: Do you have plans for dinner?

* * *

ADJUSTING her apron over her new white eyelet sundress, MJ felt prettier than she had in a long time. Going into St. Augustine, a small city just 20 minutes from Primrose, Whitney and Ever, along with their close friend Bea, had treated her to a day out. They went for pedicures, enjoyed lunch at an amazing Mexican restaurant called the Blue Corn, took her to their favorite shops, where they convinced her to buy the sundress she was wearing, and they ended the day at the farmer's market. All the fresh produce, local meats, and dairy along with beautiful preserves made MJ think of her grandmother and the beautiful meals she made, always ending with decadent homemade apple pie. Stirring the gravy on the stove, her mashed potatoes were already done, and the roast chicken rested on the cutting board ready to be carved. With her grandmother's apple pie recipe memorized, she had just checked on the oven when a knock sounded at her door.

Quickly removing her apron, she smoothed out her dress, glancing quickly at her reflection in the front entrance mirror, fluffing up the waves of her hair and dabbing at the bead of sweat that had formed on her brow from hovering over the oven. Taking a deep breath in, she opened the door of the cottage, and the breath whooshed out of her lungs. Kolt stood there, dressed in dark-wash Wranglers that stretched over his powerful thighs, a torso-hugging white t-shirt that showed off the broadness of his shoulders and strong chest and torso, and his signature cowboy hat. He had a day's worth of stubble framing his chin, and his rich brown eyes twinkled with a combination of appreciation and mischief. *Dear Lord in heaven, he's handsome.* But it wasn't just his handsome face that had her heart do a flip-flop. He held a bouquet of wildflowers in his hands, tied up tightly with a pretty yellow ribbon. No one had ever given her flowers, and the gesture was so sweet it made tears well up in her eyes. She blinked rapidly trying to stop them from briming, but it was no use as a few tears trailed down her cheeks. Noticing her emotional reaction, he reached for her, gripping her waist and pulling her into him, his strong arms wrapping around her protectively as she buried her head in his chest. He felt so gloriously warm and comforting, his masculine scent enveloping her senses with a combination of spice and leather. Kolt loosened his grip and lifted her chin to meet his baby browns, a sweet aw-shucks grin curving one side of his lips. "Hello there, Pretty Girl."

Pretty Girl. An endearment her grandparents used to call her. She smiled melancholically at the sweet memory.

"Hi," she whispered, her eyes darting to his lips, so inviting, the memory of them on hers making her heart race. His eyes searched hers, and she knew he was looking for permission, so when she gave him a small nod, he smiled, lowered his head down, tilting his hat up slightly so he could capture her lips. Although this kiss was chaste, it was as good as she remembered.

* * *

KOLT'S LIPS left Jane's, her eyes framed by long lashes fluttering open, her face flushed pink, looking so beautiful his heart skipped a beat. Releasing his hold on her, he passed the bouquet back to his other hand and held it out to her. She glanced down at the flowers, her long lashes touching the tops of her cheeks as she closed her eyes and breathed in deeply their intoxicating fragrance. Her eyes opened, the gold in them sparkling like the embers of a campfire as she said, "They're so beautiful, thank you, Kolt."

The unmistakable sizzling sound of something overflowing on the oven burner broke them apart, and Jane ran to the stove, turning off the burner quickly, a burnt smell permeating the air. Kolt followed her as she frowned at what appeared to be gravy that had boiled over onto the stovetop. He glanced down at her, her eyes glossing over with tears as she took in the mess. Putting his arm around her, she flinched at his touch, her eyes flitting to meet his with fear in their depths. *What had he done to her?* He gave her shoulder a reassuring squeeze, her eyes warming with his gesture. "No need to cry over spilled gravy. There's still enough for the two of us," he said, gesturing to the half-full saucepan. "I'll help you clean this up after it cools down a bit, okay?"

Her shoulders eased, and he let out a little chuckle. "I can tell you stories about all the messes Georgie and I made in the kitchen, including the one time I tried making grilled cheese in the oven with parmesan cheese.

And not the kind you grate, the powdered kind you sprinkle. It took months for that smell to fully leave the house."

Jane curled up her nose and let out a little giggle, tears of laughter brimming rather than sadness or fear.

"Have you ever smelled a sweaty gym sock?" he asked, loving her laughter and the bright smile on her face. "Well, that's what the house smelled like!"

Jane wrapped her arm around him, and he kissed her head affectionately. The oven timer sounded, and Jane let go, reaching for the oven mitts and opening the oven. The burning smell of the gravy was very quickly overtaken by the glorious smell of rich buttery pastry, tart apples, and floral cinnamon. Jane lifted a huge golden apple pie out of the oven, and his eyes widened with appreciation.

"Let's skip dinner and go straight to dessert," he suggested, saliva pooling at the corners of his mouth as he took in the incredible-looking pie.

Without skipping a beat, Jane cocked a playful eyebrow at him as she replied, "Don't worry, you'll get dessert."

* * *

THEY SAY the way to a man's heart is through his stomach, and if that saying is correct, she unquestionably had Kolt's heart locked and loaded. Kolt raved about the food, accepting seconds as he reached for her hand and gave it a squeeze while he praised her cooking. Her heart felt full. So appreciative of this handsome man sharing this meal with her. She had poured her heart and soul into the dinner, and he acknowledged the effort she had put in with each satisfied roll of his eyes and sigh of enjoyment. She had never experienced that kind of unbridled appreciation from a man. Definitely not from Chet. He would have slapped her, perhaps pinned her to the wall, squeezing her face tightly until her lips went blue if she had boiled over the gravy. Telling her she had ruined his meal as he unleashed his anger on her. Another broken lip or bruise on her cheek would be the result or worse. Then of course he would take off in his truck, leaving her on the floor with a stovetop full of dirty pots and uneaten food, with tears streaming down her face as he drowned his guilt at the town bar. So many meals ended like this, but here with Kolt, this was how two people who genuinely cared for each other should share a meal. With conversation, laughter, gratitude and affection.

"Are you ready for dessert?" She asked, reaching for his empty plate and getting up from the table to set their dishes in the sink.

"I'm always up for dessert," he said with a wink, making an inadvertent giggle escape her lips. She felt the heat rise to her cheeks knowing she was the one who threw out the original innuendo. Flirting was not something she had done in a long time, but with Kolt it came easily. His mischievous twinkle and their undeniable attraction to each other, giving her permission to get a little playful with him. Besides, something told her that no matter how many innuendos or flirtatious comments were passed between them, he was not going to cross the line of physicality with her unless she gave him the green light. Kolt Donahue was not the type of man to push her. He was content to let her go at her own pace. But now, looking into his gorgeous brown eyes, she wanted to throw out all inhibitions she had. All preconceived notions as to what was right or wrong and too soon, to be kicked out the door and carried off by the late spring breeze. Breaking their gaze, she looked down at the apple pie, still warm on the counter, and an idea formed in her head, making her body tingle at the thought. Reaching into the drawer, she pulled out one fork and picked up the pie. Setting down the pie and the fork at her place setting, he gave her a curious look as she took a seat and put the fork into the middle of the pie, breaking the shell of the crust and capturing it along with the sweet and spicy apple filling. With the fork loaded with homemade goodness, she lifted it to his mouth, and he smirked as he opened his mouth, taking the bite. His eyes rolled back in pure, unadulterated satisfaction, and his unrestrained reaction made the heat rise in her body. Holding out the fork to him, he took it, doing the same and feeding her a big bite of the decadent dessert.

She held her hand to her mouth as she chewed and mumbled through her mouthful, "It's so good."

He reached over and tucked a wave of her hair behind her ear, his fingers caressing the side of her cheek as he whispered, "It's perfect."

Their eyes locked, emboldened desire pooling low in her belly, as she rose from her chair and took a seat on his lap, curling her arms around his neck, her fingers playing with the soft curls at the nape. "I like you a lot, Kolt," she said, resting her forehead against his. "I'm scared though. I haven't exactly had the best experiences in relationships and well…"

He put a finger over her lips and met her eyes with nothing but sincerity reflecting back at her. "You don't have to tell me, Pretty Girl. You don't need to explain. No one is going to hurt you again. I promise you that."

MJ's heart felt full, bursting at its seams with his promise, choosing to trust her heart and knowing when she investigated Kolt's eyes that he was being forthright with her. "You are going to make me fall for you, RC," she confessed, brushing her hand through his mussed-up hair and loving the unexpected softness feathering through her fingertips.

"I hope so," he replied, offering her his sweet honest smile. "Because I'm already falling for you, Jane."

* * *

KOLT TOOK one look at Jane's expression, and he knew she had heard him, his confession, that of a man already fallen. She leaned in, her sweet mouth covering his, giving him all the answers he needed. Parting her lips, her tongue darted out, teasing his, an unbridled passion igniting with the intimacy of their exploring tongues. He lifted her, carrying her to the couch, where he settled her, still seated on his lap. They kissed for a long time, until they were breathless, panting from desire, lips swollen, and faces flushed with heat. In the throes of their make-out session, his hand had crept up her thigh, now kissing the edge of her underwear. Suddenly conscious of his roaming hand, he corrected himself, and Jane gave him an encouraging smile as she twisted her body to straddle his lap. She leaned down, his fingers tangling in her hair as she captured his lips in a scorching kiss, the heat of her core, pressing the growing ridge that was tight and painful in his jeans. *I want her.* Right now, right here, if she said, "Let's take this to bedroom", he was sure he wouldn't stop her. But Jane seemed content to kiss him long and hard, as her body rocked over his lap. She pulled her lips away, trying to catch her breath, her forehead resting on his. "You are such a great kisser," she breathed out.

"As are you," he replied, brushing his thumb gently over the kiss-bitten flesh of her lips. "I want you to know there's no pressure from me to take this further. We'll go at your pace, whatever that pace is. I just want to be with you in whatever way you feel comfortable," he said, his hands sliding up her thighs, to the edge of her dress hem and back down again.

"My mind says take it slow, but then you look at me like that and I want to go faster." She confessed, sucking in a stuttered breath.

Kolt knew exactly what she meant. The desire between them, like a spring, coiled tight and ready to let go. Cupping her face in his palms, he kissed both of her cheeks tenderly, relishing the softness of her skin against his lips and wanting nothing more than to plant kisses like that across her body. It was not lost on him that Jane had likely never experienced a man truly savoring her. True intimacy between two people who both care, respect and desire each other. Fueled by need, desire and utmost respect for the woman on his lap, he asked, "Do you trust me?" meeting her wanton gaze.

She nodded as he lifted her off his lap, setting her on her feet. He rose from the couch, his eyes locked on hers as he took her hand, leading to the bedroom. Stopping beside the bed, he reached for the hem of her dress, his gaze never leaving hers as he slowly brought the dress up past the swell of her hips, brushing the sides of her waist, making her breath come out in a stuttered staccato. She lifted her arms, letting him lift the dress over her head, leaving her before him in her simple cotton bra and panties. His eyes roamed over her body with restrained desire and reverence. The shape of her body, an hourglass with ample curves and swells — Kolt wanted to explore and map with his lips and tongue. Standing before him looking so vulnerable, he wanted to show her that this was vulnerable for him too, so he started to undress, her eyes watching each movement until he was standing before her in his boxer briefs, their vulnerabilities now matched. Two equals bared, body and soul.

Going on her tiptoes, she hooked her arms around his neck, her hazel eyes soft and sensual in their perusal. Kolt ran his fingers down her sides, tracing the slope of her hips and back up again, making her let out a moan of pleasure.

"That feels so good," she said, letting her head lull back, her long hair cascading down, brushing the tops of his large hands as he ran his fingers down over the dip of her lower back and back up over her shoulders.

Leaning in, he whispered against her ear, his hot breath causing goosebumps to rise on her skin. "I would be lying if I told you I didn't want you right now," he started, his voice coming out husky with need. "But intimacy is so much more than just sex. Tonight, I want to just touch you and kiss you, is that okay?"

Jane's eyes fluttered against his cheek as she answered breathlessly, "Yes."

* * *

TAKING HER HAND IN HIS, Kolt took a seat on the bed, his warm brown eyes caressing her before his hands did. He looked up at her with so much adoration in his eyes as he said, "You are so beautiful, Jane."

MJ had been called beautiful many times in her life. She knew she would be considered a pretty girl and attractive to most, but when Kolt said it, it made her feel truly beautiful. Not just on the outside, but from within. Kolt truly saw her, and it left her feeling raw and exposed. He leaned in, kissing the middle of her supple belly. The feel of his soft lips and scruff of his chin made goosebumps instantly rise over her skin. She tangled her fingers in his hair as he planted kisses and licks across her stomach, hip to hip, the feeling almost too much, yet not enough. Raising his chin to meet her gaze, she leaned in, capturing his lips for a sensual kiss. Groaning against her lips, she climbed on top of him, straddling his hips, feeling the evidence of his desire, thick and hard, brushing up against the needy heat of her core. She rocked once against his hardness, her body begging for the friction she knew he could give her. Before she could rock over him again, he flipped her onto her back, settling beside her, his eyes closing a moment as if trying to regain some self-control.

MJ flipped onto her side, watching him with both curiosity and uncertainty as she rested her hand on his taut stomach, feeling the rapid rise and fall under her palm. His eyes opened, and he turned his head to meet her gaze. With regained control and eyes full of affection, he splayed his hand over hers, their fingers lacing together. They lay like that for a while, just staring into each other's eyes, no words passing between them, their eyes saying far more than words could. Turning onto his side, he leaned in, kissing her shoulder. Smiling, she turned onto her stomach as he tracked his fingers over the slope of her back, tracing each vertebra and brushing her hair aside, continuing up her neck, massaging the nape and then trailing back down again. MJ's nose felt fuzzy, a combination of desire, pure bliss, and untapped lust commingling into the most remarkable sensation across her entire body. "Can I undo your bra?" he asked.

"Yes," she replied, her voice soft and breathy.

Climbing up onto his knees, he unfastened her bra, his fingertips massaging the skin, indented from the band, and he leaned down, kissing the puckered skin, making an involuntary moan escape her throat. Blazing hot kisses up and down her back, she could feel all the tension leave her body as she savored the softness of his feather-like kisses on her skin. His hands coasted over the swell of her behind, but he didn't knead the flesh, although if he did, she wouldn't have protested. Everything about his reverent touch was sensual, not sexual. After kissing every inch, he rested to the side of her as he traced languid circles on her back. She felt so relaxed, almost sleepy, as her eyes fluttered open, meeting his waiting gaze.

"Can I spend the night here with you?" he asked, his

fingertips tracing the shell of her ear, making her eyes flutter closed again.

In her blissed-out state, all she could manage was a nod. Kolt rolled off the bed, walking over to her dresser, her tired eyes tracking him. Gesturing to it, she nodded, and he opened the top dresser drawer, pulling out a sleep shirt and walking it over to her. She rolled over, holding her open bra tightly to her chest. She sat up on the side of the bed, and he handed her the shirt. Not thinking, she dropped the bra, letting it slide down her arms, and she heard Kolt's breath suck in as he quickly turned, allowing her to put on the sleeping shirt. When he was sure she was covered, he took her hand, leading her to the wash-room, where they brushed their teeth, sharing her tooth-brush with him, and he gave her privacy to take care of her needs before his own. Climbing into the cool sheets of her bed, she covered herself with the comforter, relaxed mind and body, making her start to drift off as soon as her head hit the pillow. Before she entered dreamland, she felt his heat at her back and his strong muscular arm pulling her in flush to his body. Lost in a world where she felt special, cherished, and cared for by a man for the first time in her life, she drifted off into a dreamless sleep.

CHAPTER 7

Waking with Jane in his arms was so much better than he could have imagined. Her soft curves molded to his sharp edges as he spooned her, his hand resting on her belly. Her auburn hair tickled his face, and he brushed it aside, letting it cascade over the pillow like a blaze of fire over the white linens. Nuzzling his nose into the nape of her neck, he breathed in deeply, the sweet smell of her intoxicating him like the wild-flower bouquet he picked for her. Everything about this woman ignited passion, desire, emotion, and feelings he had never felt before. Telling her last night that he was falling for her only scratched the surface of how he was feeling for Jane. He knew irrevocably, with clarity and surety, that he had never felt like this for any other woman before. His heart had imprinted on hers with that first kiss, and he was now hopelessly in love with Jane.

Her warm body stirred, and she pushed all that luscious softness back against him, making an involuntary groan escape his lips. Although last night he had appeared to be the pinnacle of strength and restraint, his mind was in overdrive, his desire to let his fingers, lips and tongue explore the secret caverns of her body almost too overwhelming to take. And yet, he held back his own desires as he wanted her to feel cherished, rather than claimed. Last night he had proven to her that he could be trusted, and until she said the words "I'm ready", he wasn't going to explore that side of their newfound intimacy. Not this soon, not yet.

Tracing featherlike kisses along her shoulder, he felt her hand come over his, intertwining their fingers as she pressed his hand against her stomach and a sigh escaped her lips.

"Good morning," he whispered against her cheek. "How'd you sleep?"

"So good," she replied, her voice still laden with groggy thickness. "I like feeling you next to me," she said, turning to face him as he lay back against the mattress. Finding a groove on his chest to rest her head and with her hand resting over his heart, she added. "You're so warm."

He let out a chuckle, his deep tenor reverberating through his body. "I am a natural source of heat," he replied, pulling her hand up and kissing her palm, noticing for the first time the raised skin on her wrist. A scar running about three inches from the base of her wrist. The line was pink, a deeper shade than her skin tone, and looked new, like it had happened within the past year. "What happened here?" he asked, smoothing his fingertips over the scar again.

Jane's face morphed from contented bliss to despondency, her eyes full of uncertainty, but she didn't pull her wrist away.

"He did this to you, didn't he?" Kolt asked, meeting her eyes with concern.

The solemn look on her face was her answer, so he raised her wrist to his lips, gently tracing the scar with kisses, then rested her palm back over his heart. With her eyes fixed on him, she said, "Thank you for last night. No one has ever cared for me like that before."

"You deserve to be cared for, Jane," he said, lifting her chin to press his lips to hers. She sighed into his mouth, and he pulled her tight to him, loving the warmth and comfort of holding her in his arms. As they lay there together, he couldn't help but let his head spin with questions. Questions he needed to know the answers to if they were going to start a relationship, but where to begin. "Jane, I know you've been to hell and back, and I know you've been guarded, rightfully so, since you came to Primrose. I appreciate the bits and pieces that you've shared with me so far, but I want you to know that no matter what you share with me, I won't judge you. I need you to understand that." he said. "I have never believed that our histories define us. If we want to start a relationship, which I hope you do, I need to know more."

MJ LET OUT A LONG, painful exhale. What Kolt was asking her to do was going to rip her open, gut her and expose all the darkness. Years of abuse, years of feeling unworthy of living, years of feeling like she was unlovable. Years that

Chet isolated her, controlled her, abused her physically, emotionally, and mentally, taking advantage of her affections all the time masking it with the word love. What she had experienced with Chet wasn't love. She knew that now.

Meeting Kolt's beseeching gaze, she wondered if she would find that kind of love with Kolt. The kind of love she deserved and wanted for the rest of her life. If she were going to experience the kind of love she desired with the man holding her right now, she needed to open fully to him. *But where to start?*

Shifting to bring herself to a sitting position, Kolt propped her pillows up against the headboard as she pulled the covers over her legs, and Kolt positioned himself next to her, his expression one of patience. Looking down at her hands, he reached over, intertwining his fingers with hers as she began. "I met Chet at the beginning of 12th grade. He was three years older than me, so 20 at that time. I knew him well as our town's golden boy and the son of a prominent local businessman. I was so flattered that he even noticed me, and soon after he showed interest we started dating. At first, he was kind and sweet, good to my grandparents and said all the right things, giving them and me false security that he was going to love me and take care of me. Then, when they passed away in a car accident, he was there for me, by my side through it all. I felt loved, and he moved into the farmhouse with me, promising to help me out financially and maintain our family farm." She explained, swallowing hard. "During this time, I lost so many friends, thinking the reason was all the responsibilities that were now on my plate, but slowly I noticed that he was pulling me from them, and he had been for years, isolating me from the outside world." Kolt breathed in, placing his other hand over hers, letting her know he was taking in each word. "The first time he hit me, I was just emptying the dishwasher and his favorite coffee cup slipped out of my hand, fell to the floor and broke. He said nothing, rising from the kitchen table and coming towards the mess. I thought he was going to help me clean it up, but instead, he punched me in the jaw. I will never forget the snap of my neck and the sharp pain that spread across my face. The shock was too…" she sucked in a breath. "That was just the first."

Kolt lifted her hand to his mouth and kissed the back of her hand. "I'm so sorry."

She gave him a grateful look as she continued. "Chet worked on the oil fields up north, being gone for several weeks at a time, which would give me reprieve and time to recover from his beatings. After one particularly bad night, the night he broke my wrist, sending me to the hospital, he must have felt concerned that I was going to leave him, because the next morning I found him in Prairie's box stall with a shotgun. He said that if I ever tried to leave him, he would shoot my horse." She said, her voice cracking with emotion as her lashes fluttered and a tear rolled down her cheek. "Prairie Prestige is all I have left of my grandparents. He has been my horse from the day he was born, and I belong to him as much as he belongs to me. All I have is Prairie."

"What about your grandparents' farm? Did they not

leave it to you?" Kolt asked, reaching over, and brushing away her tears with his thumb.

"Chet is paying the mortgage. He took it over and convinced me to transfer all financing to his name." She said. "I know that was a stupid move on my part, but I didn't know how I was going to pay it and I was sure Chet, and I would marry and raise a family on that farm." she said looking down with shame, her voice breaking. "I truly thought he loved me."

Kolt's heart was ready to break with her words. Jane had been through so much, bruised, broken both in body and spirit. But she was here, bravely fleeing the situation and trying to start a new life for herself with the one and only thing that mattered to her most, her horse. He understood the connection completely, the trust and love between animal and human. Seeing it every day during therapy. Feeling it with Stetson. Animals had the power not only to heal someone but to save them. Prairie Prestige was her savior, and from what she was telling him, she was his.

He put his arms around her as she cried, and pulled her into him, enveloping her in all his warmth and protection. Swallowing down the painful lump that formed in his throat after hearing her story, he wanted to free her from all the pain she had been through, but he knew he couldn't. All he could do was love her the way she deserved to be loved. And that was exactly what he was going to do.

Lifting her chin to meet his eyes, he kissed each cheek, the saltiness of her tears on his lips. She closed her eyes, let out a sigh, then slowly opened them to meet his gaze.

With conviction he promised her, "You are safe here in Primrose. I will protect you, and I will protect Prairie Prestige."

A melancholy smile tugged at her lips as she replied, "I know you will." Curling herself around his torso, he brushed her hair from her face, letting the soft strands slip through his fingers as a question crossed his mind and he smiled, curious as to her answer. "What is your real name? As much as I like Just Jane, I know that's not it and I would love to know."

"It's Mary Jane Kasper," she answered with a smile. "But since I was little, everyone called me MJ."

"Nice to finally meet you, MJ," Kolt said, brushing a sweet kiss to her lips and then meeting her gaze. "If you don't mind, you will always be Jane to me."

It was Rodeo weekend with St. Augustine hosting in conjunction with their annual Summer Fair. MJ was buzzing with excitement as she arrived at the fairgrounds, parking next to Ben and Ever with their eleven-year-old twin girls, Violet and Poppy, and seven-year-old Son, Luke, in tow. Hayden, Whitney, and the kids would be meeting them later for the rodeo. It had been years since MJ had been to a country fair, and she wanted to see, hear, and taste everything. The event she was most excited about other than the rodeo, of course, was the Arabian horse show happening this afternoon. Sweet memories of showing Prairie, competing in Western Pleasure, and showmanship classes, taking home ribbon after ribbon, flooded her. So proud to show off her beautiful horse and abilities on horseback as her grandparents watched from the grandstand beaming with pride.

Agreeing to meet up with everyone before the rodeo started, she made her way to the corner of the fairgrounds near the stables where the horse show was just starting. She found a spot on the grandstand and watched as the riders entered the ring, decked out in flashy western gear, showing off their horses groomed to pristine perfection. Watching as they walked the perimeter of the ring, the ringmaster directed them to jog, then lope, taking note of the gait and smoothness with which they transitioned. They noted how the horses responded to their riders' cues and how responsive they were. As she watched, MJ remembered a conversation with her grandfather after her first horse show when she and Prairie didn't place in the class. She had been disappointed; the judge saying her horse was special, but she needed more practice. Her grandfather told her that showing your horse is a partnership. *A partnership between you and your horse. You and Prairie have a connection, a trust that many don't have. You just need to build your confidence and know that Prairie has you. He will always have you. He isn't going to let you down. So don't let him down.* From that conversation forward, there was not a class that Prairie didn't place, and that was because she and Prairie were now a team. Watching as the placements were announced and little girls decked out in western gear handed out ribbons to the winners, MJ itched to be in that ring again. Prairie Prestige was special, as strong and vibrant as any of the class winners.

Perhaps she could show again. Perhaps Kolt could help her.

MJ smiled as heat ran through her body thinking of him. Last week he was in her bed, confessing his feelings for her and showing her how much he cared. *Am I ready for this? The kind of love he can bring to my life.* She knew the answer was yes. When she thought about her grandparents and the love they shared, she wanted that too. Someone she could sit on the front porch with, holding hands, their hair greying, weathered lines on their faces. A friend, a companion, a teammate, and a lover. Someone who always made her feel loved and desired and protected her heart. Something in her gut told her that Kolt was the type of man who could give that to her.

She ran her fingertips over the scar on her wrist, the bitter memory of that day still so fresh in her mind. How Chet was so apologetic after he lost control, his words of forgiveness hollow and meaningless as he drove her to the hospital and begged for her to lie as to how it happened. He was often sorry afterwards, pleading with her not to leave him. But so many times, she was left on the floor, bloodied, bruised, and violated while he took off in his truck and drowned his guilt at the local bar. She squeezed her eyes shut at that thought. How his anger often fueled his arousal, and he always took what he wanted, even if she wasn't ready or said no. All the times she was left with tears streaming down her face, feeling like a shell, empty and discarded.

She took a deep cleansing breath to try to push back the dark memories. She thought about Kolt, his impossibly handsome smile and those brown eyes that could melt her with the smallest of glances. How it felt to be held by him and how he held back his own desires, so he could cherish her and give to her selflessly. Their night together made her feel coveted, and she wanted more.

Sighing, she glanced towards the ring, realizing she had missed an entire class with her daydreams and glanced at her watch. It was almost time for her to meet the Hastings at the rodeo grandstand. She climbed down from her perch and made her way through the fairgoers, starting to gather in anticipation for the main event. Ben's tall, hulking figure came into view as she navigated through the excited crowd to reach them. Shortly, the gates were opened, and they shuffled into the arena together, finding a row in the middle with a good view. MJ was buzzing with anxious energy, grasping her hands, and wringing them with the anticipation of seeing her Roadside Cowboy.

Whitney was seated beside her, and she gave her shoulder a playful nudge. "Are you excited to see Kolt?"

"I am," she replied with a wide grin.

"I noticed his truck in our driveway last week and again the following morning, so I assume things are going well with our resident cowboy?" Whitney asked curiously.

MJ felt a blush creep up her neck and settle in her cheeks, knowing something would eventually be said. It wasn't like they were hiding the fact that he spent the night, and she was living on Whitney and Hayden's property.

"No need to tell me anything." She said, putting her arm around her and giving her shoulder a squeeze. "Know that both Hayden and I are happy for you. I have gotten to know Kolt pretty well over the years, and he is truly a good man. What you see is what you get. A true honest to goodness gentleman."

"I've fallen for him." MJ confessed with a whisper just loud enough for Whitney to hear. "I know it's crazy since I've only been in Primrose two months, but when I think of the future, I see him in it."

"Then that's love." Whitney said, bringing her hand to her heart. "Sometimes, you need to experience what love isn't to truly recognize what love is."

Whitney's words settled in her heart. *Am I in love with Kolt?* If anyone understood that, it was Whitney. With a decision being made, her lips tugged up into a slow smile. *I am going all in on Kolt.* No looking back, only forward, letting him show me the love I deserve.

The music started, the cheers of the crowd igniting as a couple of rodeo clowns entered the ring, entertaining the onlookers with their antics. The timed events were first, ending with Kolt's events: steer wrestling, tie down roping and team roping. They watched, cheered, and laughed, enjoying each event in anticipation of seeing Kolt compete.

"There he is!" Ever exclaimed, pointing towards the gate.

MJ's eyes darted to where she was pointing, and indeed there he was, entering the ring on Stetson, looking like the sexiest, most confident cowboy she had ever seen. Dressed in his signature tan cowboy hat, a light blue western shirt that hugged every glorious angle of his upper body and arms, and Wranglers that molded over his thick thighs, she bit her lip, feeling her breath catch at the sight of him. He sat high in the saddle, and his eyes combed the crowd as Stetson paced, anxious for his first round. Spotting them, their eyes met across the distance, his lips curled up in a grin and he tipped his hat with a nod towards her. MJ felt her heart flutter with the gesture as he brought his focus from her back to his event. Entering the loading gate, he positioned Stetson, readied them, his body noticeably vibrating with anticipation even across the arena.

Ben leaned forward, resting his elbows on his thighs as he said, "Kolt has his game face on. Let's see if he can beat his best time."

"Next up Kolt Donahue from Primrose, Manitoba," the announcer introduced. "He came close to winning this competition last year. Let's see if he can take home the buckle this year."

The gate opened, Kolt and Stetson charged forward and quickly caught up to the steer. At breakneck speed, he flew off Stetson, gripped the horns of the steer and wrestled it to the ground.

"That's it Kolt!" Hayden exclaimed, the spectators cheering loudly as everyone rose to their feet waiting for the announcer to reveal his time.

"4.2 seconds! That's a new record for Donahue!"

The crowd exploded, MJ feeling like she was going to burst with happiness for him. Everyone took their seats, watching as three more cowboys competed trying to beat his time. But they couldn't even touch it, and Kolt was declared the winner. He did a victory lap on Stetson and came around again, stopping short in front of their group, his eyes meeting MJ's as he blew her a kiss. All eyes turned to her, her cheeks taking on a rosy hue as she put her hand to her lips and blew a kiss back.

"Looks like Donahue won't be celebrating alone tonight." The announcers said. "Sorry ladies, looks like our local cowboy is taken." Disappointed groans sifted through the crowd.

Kolt flashed her a swoon-worthy grin, then rode out of the ring, her heart following him as he went.

"CONGRATS, KOLT!" a fellow cowboy from Alberta said as he stopped him after his last competition. Kolt knew Thatcher Stevens well, a fellow roper from Smoky Lake, Alberta, who he had competed against in team roping. Thatcher was younger than him, in his mid-twenties, a real firecracker and cocky as hell. He was well known for doing the rounds with the buckle bunnies, as most of the young bucks did when they realized there were perks to rodeoing. Kolt would be lying if he said he didn't partake in those perks in his younger years, but since he entered his 30s, the scene had grown old with him wanting more than just a little post-rodeo romp. "Who was that pretty redhead up in the stands?" Thatcher asked, his thumbs in the loops of his jeans. "Is that your girl?"

"She is." Kolt replied proudly, narrowing his eyes at Thatcher, wondering where his questioning was going.

Thatcher removed his cowboy hat and scratched his head, a look of confusion on his face. "She looks awfully familiar, but I can't seem to place her. She looks so much like a girl a buddy of mine was dating back home," he added, his eyes drifted up to meet Kolt's. "Is her name MJ by chance?" he asked, his lips curling up in a knowing grin.

The hair on the back of Kolt's neck pricked up, and a feeling of foreboding washed over him with his pointed question. Schooling his facial expressions, he answered, "No, it's not."

He shook his head and let out a low laugh. "Funny, she looks just like her," he said with a shrug. "Well, congrats, and we'll see you in September in Hanna," he said as he clapped Kolt on the back and disappeared into the crowd.

Smoky Lake, Alberta. Was that where she was from? Is Thatcher friends with Chet? Kolt felt sick to his stomach, knowing he needed to tell Jane about his conversation with Thatcher. As much as he didn't want to break her bubble of anonymity and security, she needed to know. *But how am I going to tell her and not scare her off? How do I keep her from running scared?*

"Get your ass to the ring, Donahue," a fellow cowboy shouted from across the gate. "Champion Ceremony is about to start, and they're waiting for you."

He tipped his hat in acknowledgement and entered the ring, cheers of a champion's welcome awaiting him.

* * *

WAITING for Kolt on the sidelines, MJ's body was nearly vibrating with the need to wrap herself around him. Watching Kolt compete was exhilarating, and she was so proud of him, winning both Steer Wrestling and taking first place in the Team Roping Competition, a double buckle winner.

Her eyes searched the crowd of lingering spectators, trying to spot him. When the crowd parted, there he was, her handsome cowboy, dusty, dirty, and looking like a dream. Spotting them, he swaggered over, a humble "aw-shucks" grin planted firmly on his face as he approached her. The look in his eyes made her breath catch as he reached her, his large hand tangling in the soft waves of her hair as he pulled her close, his long strong body melding into her softness. He smelled like a combination of horse, hay, sweat and leather, and the intoxicating combination made her head spin.

"Hey, there, Pretty Girl," he said, his arm securely around her waist, her chin high, meeting the playful twinkle in his brown eyes.

"Hi" she replied, not caring who was watching them. "You were amazing today."

He responded with a modest shrug. "I may have shown off a bit for someone special in the stands."

MJ smiled, bringing her bottom lip between her teeth as her eyes drifted slowly to his lips and then back to his swoony stare. Kolt didn't miss the gesture and leaned down, brushing his lips to hers, making her knees weak as he kissed her tenderly.

A throat cleared, and they pulled apart, turning to face the Hastings, all of them, eyes brimming with amusement and wide smiles on their faces. Ever spoke first. "So, I'm assuming from that little display of PDA you two are finally together?"

"Is Jane your girlfriend?" Eight-year-old Beckett asked, his hands on his hips.

"Yeah, because that was gross." 7-year-old Bodhi said, sticking out his tongue. "Mom and Dad kiss like that all the time," he added, scrunching up his nose.

Everyone started laughing as Hayden pulled Whitney in, planting a kiss on her lips, all three of their boys making puking noises.

Kolt looked down at her imploring with his eyes for an answer, and she nodded, as she wanted that label more than anything. The sweetest smile curled his lips as he turned to Beckett, answering, "Yes, Jane is my girlfriend."

Becket gave him a thumbs up with a cheesy grin, making everyone laugh. Kolt glanced down at her, his eyes dancing with happiness as he pulled her in for a hug.

CHAPTER 8

Kolt and Jane meandered hand in hand through the crowds, stopping at vendors perusing their wares, carnival alley and checking out the midway. As they combed the fair offerings, Kolt fielded shouts of congratulations, pats on the back and the odd rodeo fan asking him for a selfie.

"You're a bit of a celebrity around here." Jane commented with an amused grin.

"I've been around the circuit for a while, so people know me. Plus, with St. Augustine being as good as my hometown, I get a lot of local support." He replied modestly.

"You're like a hometown hero," she said, squeezing his hand.

"Nah. Just a regular guy that's dumb enough to wrestle a steer," he replied, with a chuckle.

"Well, you looked super-hot doing it." She added, cocking an eyebrow his way.

"Oh, I did, did I?" he asked, pulling her into him, his hands settling on her waist and massaging through the light cotton of her dress, itching to feel the softness of her skin under his fingertips.

The sound of a local country band started playing from the bandshell, and Kolt could see couples gathering on the makeshift outdoor dance floor. "Come with me," he said, leading her to the dance floor.

The sun had just set, and strings of fairy lights criss-crossed the space overhead, adding to the twinkle of stars pushing through the wispy clouds and glow of the city lights. The nighttime breeze was warm and inviting, and Kolt twirled her around, making her knee-length cotton sundress spin before he brought her flush with his body. They danced with him, spinning her around the dance floor, making her giggle ring like the sweet sound of church bells on Sunday morning. *God, I love that laugh. That infectious smile. The sheer joy in her eyes. So Beautiful. So different from two months ago when she arrived in Primrose.*

A female lead singer stepped to the microphone. A classic country tune filling the air, that Kolt remembered was one of his mother's favorites from Martina McBride. *With a broken wing, she carries her dreams;* the words speaking to the woman in his arms. The woman he was starting to piece back together. He could see it happening with every little moment they spent together. A bridge of trust slowly being built between them.

His mind drifted to his conversation with Thatcher Stevens. Thatcher knew who she was, and he now knew he was from her Alberta hometown. His mind reeled.

Should I tell her about my conversation with Thatcher? Would it make her take two steps back, rather than two steps forward with me, or would it make her retreat altogether? Is our new relationship strong enough for her to stay? I don't know. Looking down at the beautiful woman in his arms, he couldn't imagine seeing that fear in her eyes again.

Holding her hand to his heart, her eyes slowly drifted up to meet his with so much affection and trust. *My broken bird, my Jane. I am not going to lose her.* His chest filling with fear that she might run, he made a quick decision. *For now, Jane doesn't need to know.*

NIGHTMARES FOR MJ always started the same, her backing into a corner, Chet looming over her, his dark mean eyes squinting at her through narrow slits, his face flaming red with anger and his voice a sinister growl. In her dreams, she would relive times he hurt her, either by beating or defiling her. She never knew which way it was going to go wishing she could control the memories that would spin through her head like a tornado ripping through a trailer park. Leaving rubble, twisted metal, and shards of everything she held dear around her. She could feel his heavy hand strike her face, the burn of air hitting broken and bloodied skin and the weight of him on top of her, pinning her in place, knowing she couldn't fight back if she tried. Chet was a large man, six foot two, two hundred and thirty pounds, a huge contrast to her petite five-foot five frame, and he could easily overpower her. She felt sharp tears pierce her eyes, and a gasping sob followed in quick succession as she screamed, "No, Chet!"

"Jane." a rich soothing voice said next to her, a warm hand on her shoulder. "Wake up, Pretty girl."

Pretty Girl. That's what Grandpa called you; that's what Kolt calls you. Two men you love and trust. A gentle hand caressed her arm, and her eyes fluttered open, feeling the wetness on her pillow and the clamminess of her skin. She swallowed, trying to speak, her voice painfully raw with emotion.

"You had a nightmare." Kolt said softly, next to her ear as he pulled her into him, his strong arm coming around her protectively with her back to his front. "I'm here Jane, he can't get you. I'll keep you safe."

MJ started to sob, her consciousness still lingering between wake and sleep, exhaustion, frustration, embarrassment pulling her under as she buried her face in her pillow and cried.

"Pretty Girl, come here, let me hold you." Kolt said as she turned in his arms and found her place in the groove of his body while her body shook with her sobs against his warm skin. "I got you," he continued to coo, as he stroked her hair and circled the shell of her ear with his fingertips. Before long, her eyes felt heavy again, and her stuttered tears subsided as she drifted back to sleep, the nightmares being cast to the shadows for now.

* * *

KOLT WOKE THE NEXT MORNING, sunshine streaming through the open curtains of his bedroom window with shadows dancing across the wall from the breeze rustling the leaves in the trees that surrounded the farmhouse. It had been two weeks since the rodeo, he and Jane spending more nights together than apart. His bed felt empty without her now, and he knew she felt secure in his arms. Despite their sleeping arrangements, they had yet to take their intimacy to a sexual level, even though he knew it was coming. He could feel the unfettered desire in her kisses, the way she looked at him with not only a growing love but a passion that was ready to overflow. But there was something holding her back, and after last night he was sure he knew what it was. Last night she had another nightmare, not the first he had experienced since they started sleeping together, and he knew it wouldn't be the last. Each one was painful to watch, her inability to distinguish between her subconscious and reality in that moment. The screams, the fearful cries and his name uttered from her lips. *Chet.* She had spoken his name so many times in her sleep, and each time it was laced with fear. The monster she couldn't shake and couldn't be erased by Kolt's own loving and gentle touches. The realization of that caused a painful lump of emotion to form in his throat that constricted his breath and made him want to weep. *If only I could protect her from the memories and take away all the pain from the past.*

He swallowed hard, sifting his fingers through her silky hair with Jane curled around him, her soft, supple body molding perfectly to his. Not until he held her did her crying stop and her breathing even, allowing her to fall back into a dreamless sleep. As he listened to her steady breaths, he stared into the darkness, shaken by her screams and subsequent tears, trying to get his head around it all. He knew she had been beaten and now, after last night's horrific dream, he was sure she had been… he couldn't even say the word. The thought, too disturbing and painful to think of.

Jane needed to talk to someone, and he needed to figure out how to help her. *Perhaps Georgie?* His sister, although she worked mostly with children, was a licensed therapist. She had so many certifications behind her that he was sure she could help Jane or at the very least recommend someone that could.

Jane stirred in his arms, a low groggy moan escaping her lips, her warm body shifting around his, like he was her body pillow. Her eyes fluttered open, and she looked up, meeting his gaze.

"Good morning, Pretty Girl," he whispered, feigning a smile to cover the worry that wracked him.

"Good morning." She replied, carefully surveying his face, her brows knitting together in concern. "You look like you haven't slept much. Did I snore?"

"No, you purr kind of like a kitten when you sleep," he said with a wink, his gaze washing over with wariness. "But you did have another nightmare last night."

Jane's face instantly reddened, embarrassment clouding her eyes, as she asked. "Oh, God. What did I say?"

"You screamed, "No, Chet,"" he replied.

She buried her face for a moment and then looked up into his eyes, fear now overtaking the embarrassment as she said simply. "He used to get rough with me."

"Sexually?" he asked.

She nodded, adding, "Chet didn't understand the word "no"."

Kolt sucked in a breath, his eyes going to the ceiling as he ran a hand over his stubbled face, feeling anger and disgust rise in his chest. Consent was the number one rule in intimacy. They even taught it to middle schoolers these days, and the fact that he not only beat her but took her against her will was almost too much to take in.

Jane unraveled herself from his body, turning away and sitting on the edge of the bed, burying her face in her hands, her shoulders shaking with her tears as she said, "I understand if this is all too much for you. I know I'm damaged."

"No, Pretty Girl, no," he said, climbing over to sit down beside her. "I don't look at you and see someone that's damaged. I see someone who survived a very volatile and toxic situation and was brave enough to get away. I'm not going to lie and tell you that it isn't painful to see you hurting and to think about what he did to you, but you're not damaged to me. I do, however, think you need to talk to someone about it though. Someone other than me."

"I wouldn't even begin to know who," she said, shaking her head and wiping the wetness from her cheeks with the palm of her hand. "I honestly just want the nightmares to stop."

"I think you should talk to Georgie," he said, reaching for her hand and lacing his fingers through hers. "She's a licensed therapist, and she may be able to help you." Jane's eyes met his apprehension in their depths. "Why don't you go riding with her and you can just talk? Georgie is the best listener."

"Do you really think she could help?" She asked, leaning her head on his shoulder.

"I do," he said, putting his arm around her. *I do.*

* * *

MJ PULLED up to the barn on the Donahue farm and took a deep cleansing breath. She had given Kolt the okay to arrange this with his sister, and now as she sat here in her truck, she was regretting it. Therapy meant revealing everything. Even more than she had revealed to Kolt. He knew the vague truth. More reading between the lines than actual circumstances and events. Today was going to open old wounds, but the reality was that she had no choice but to try.

Just go in there and feel things out, she said, giving herself an internal pep talk. *You like Georgie.* Georgie was fun, smart, effervescent and had been kind and welcoming to her. If Kolt trusted her, surely, she could trust her too.

Georgie appeared in the doorway of the barn waving at her as Jane climbed out of her truck.

"Hey," she said, offering her a caring smile and leaning in to give her a hug. Jane leaned into the comfort that surrounded her, and she let out the long breath she had been holding. "It's all going to be okay." Georgie whispered softly as she released their embrace and held MJ out at arm's length. "I can promise you that," she said with sincerity in her brown eyes. MJ's shoulders eased, some of the nervous tension releasing with her comforting words as Georgie said, "Let's get the horses ready. I know just the place we can go to talk."

They made short work of saddling the horses, and MJ followed Georgie down the driveway, Prairie striding next to Georgie's dappled grey Arabian mare. Reaching the gravel road that led to their farm, they turned in the opposite direction of the main road and rode quietly for a long time, side by side, matching pace and enjoying the warmth of the June day.

"That's the end of our property right over there. There's a small creek that separates our property from the Isley's, where my best friend, Brooks, grew up." Georgie said, pointing off to a line of trees and a noticeable crevasse that separated their field from the neighbor's. MJ nodded. "Kolt made mention that you have a farm in Alberta that your grandparents left you."

"Yeah, about five miles outside of Smoky Lake, Alberta. It's small, though. Not like Prairie Sky or Donahue Farms. Only a small acreage, with a farmhouse, shed row barn, and a few acres of pastureland. The farmhouse is old and in dire need of repair. My grandparents wanted to renovate it, but never had the chance." MJ said.

"When did they pass away?" Georgie asked.

"I was 19, so 4 years ago." MJ replied. "They had a car accident, lost control on a gravel road a few miles from the farm. Their car rolled and hit a tree. They didn't survive the crash."

"Oh, Jane, I'm so sorry." She said, giving her a sympathetic look. "Did you have any family there to help you through it?"

"No, I only ever had my grandparents. My mother

died giving birth to me, so my grandparents raised me," she replied. "I had a great childhood though, and my grandparents loved me so much. They weren't the richest people, but they were rich in blessings. They worked so hard to provide me with opportunities."

"I like that." Georgie said, looking towards the edge of their property and turning her horse to follow the creek on the property line, quiet contemplation settling between them, until Georgie broke the silence. "So, you were all alone after they passed?"

"No, I had a boyfriend. Chet and I had been dating for two years when they passed, and he stood beside me through it."

"Tell me about Chet," she urged.

MJ swallowed hard, remembering how much of a comfort he was after the accident as she grieved. Such a contrast from the man he turned out to be. That time was the calm before the hurricane. A storm that ripped her life apart as she knew it.

"I met Chet when I was 17. He was well known in my town as the guy that all the girls wanted. He was handsome and charming and came from a well-known family. I was completely infatuated with him, and he could have had anyone, but he wanted me. A quiet farm girl from the middle of nowhere." She shared with melancholy. "We started dating, and by the time I graduated, he was my whole world. He seemed to be kind to my grandparents, although I was sure my grandfather didn't like him. I figured he was just being protective, but later I wondered if he knew something I didn't know." MJ shared with a sigh. "I'm sure there were red flags, but Chet knew what to say and when to say it, and I stupidly bought everything he was selling."

"You weren't stupid, Jane," Georgie said. "You were young, impressionable, and it sounds like he gave you no reason to think he would be anything other than what he had shown you already. Did you have any other friends you could count on during that time?"

"Not really. Most of the friends I had grown up with left our town very quickly after graduation, either pursuing college or university or wanting to see what one of the big cities had to offer them. Not many stayed, and those that did sort of moved on from their friendships with me after my grandparents passed. Chet didn't like me going out without him, so, looking back, I think that got old for my friends."

"So, he kind of isolated you then?" Georgie asked. "Limited your contact with others."

"Yes, in retrospect, that was exactly what he was doing." She replied.

They discussed her relationship with Chet that whole afternoon, the conversation a hard one to relive. Georgie had a way of getting her to open up to her, and knowing that whatever she shared was confidential, she felt comfortable being candid. Georgie gave her a shoulder to cry on when she needed it, and she felt a trust and camaraderie forming between them that she had never had before. Like Georgie was not only her therapist, but a friend. By the end of their ride, MJ felt lighter. Like this unbearably heavy weight was being lifted.

Returning from their ride, they removed the saddles and saddle pads, brushed down their horses and settled them into box stalls when they were done. Jane was latching the door of the box stall, and when she turned, Kolt was there leaning against the cased opening of the barn, looking so damn handsome her heart skipped a beat. Georgie looked between them and turned to MJ asking, "Same time next week?"

MJ nodded, her attention drifting back to the gorgeous cowboy waiting for her.

"I'll leave you two alone." Georgie said with a knowing smile as she walked towards the exit and gave her brother a nod, patting his shoulder.

Kolt flashed Georgie a grateful smile and then turned the smile to MJ, a combination of concern and affection in his eyes. She rushed to him, the need to feel his arms around her palpable. Curling her arms around his back, her palms on his shoulder blades, she rested her cheek on his chest, inhaling the spice of his cologne, his familiar smell a protective shield around her heart. "Thank you." She said, looking up and meeting his compassionate brown eyes.

"What for?" he chuckled, planting a kiss on her nose.

"For suggesting I talk to Georgie. I know it was just one session, but somehow it all feels less heavy now."

"I'm so glad," he said, leaning down and planting a soft, sweet kiss on her lips before he pulled back and asked. "Do you have plans tonight?"

"No," she replied, cocking a curious brow at him. "What do you have in mind?"

"There's a utility road that leads to our meadow, and I was wondering if you would like to sleep under the stars tonight. Prairie is fine here overnight, and it's supposed to be clear," he said, caressing her cheek.

Our meadow, she smiled as she asked, "Are we camping?"

"Kind of." he replied, taking her hand, and leading her towards his truck. Dropping the tailgate, he revealed a thick camping-style air mattress in the bed of the truck.

"I have plenty of blankets and pillows in the backseat, and I even packed us a picnic," he said, rubbing her back. "What do you think?"

Jane felt so touched by everything he had planned. A date under the stars. It was both thoughtful and so romantic the starry-eyed girl in her was swooning. There was only one possible answer to his question. "I think this is amazing, Kolt. But could I take a shower and change before we go?"

"Of course," he replied, following her to her truck, opening the door for her as she reached into the cab to grab her bag. "Just go on inside and do what you need to do. I'm going to grab a few more things we may need, and I'll see you inside shortly."

LETTING the hot water of the shower roll over her body, MJ relished the comforting feeling as her mind wandered to the events of the day. The therapy session with Georgie, more like confiding in a good friend than a therapist, was exactly what she needed. Having kept tight-lipped about her past, staying guarded with only sharing tidbits was starting to get difficult. She was done keeping secrets, done telling herself that she was okay, just because she got away from Chet. The scars were deep, but maybe if she talked about them, they could start to heal. Kolt had been right, and she was so grateful to have him in her corner. It had been three quiet months here in Primrose. Three months where she could give herself permission to be happy. Happier than she had ever been. Primrose, an unexpected and wonderful sanctuary. A place that made her happy and feel safe. A place Kolt led her to.

Kolt. Just saying his name made her heart flutter wildly and desire pool low in her belly. Tonight, she and Kolt were going to be alone under the stars, just the two of them and the prairie night sky. *Is tonight the night?* Her heart rate quickened when she thought about being with him. He had more than proven himself to her, that she could trust him and that he would treat her with care and gentleness. They had spent weeks building an intimacy that some couples never find, and he had been more than patient. *It is time.*

After washing her hair and body quickly, she climbed out of the shower, reaching for a towel and drying herself off. Pressing her dripping hair, she glanced in the mirror; her face rosy and flushed as she thought about giving Kolt all of herself tonight. The sensation of his calloused hands touching her skin, coasting over her curves, and finding her most intimate place where she pulsed for him. The thought of seeing all of him, bare and naked before her, made her bite her lip. Kolt was a beautiful man, his body carved by hard work and hard riding. Sometimes as she lay in bed with him, she found herself tracing the edges of his taut frame, wondering what it would feel like to have all that power hovering over her, pressing her hot and heavy into the mattress. Having felt the evidence of his desire for her many times while they slept in the same bed with their bodies curled around each other. It was not lost on her that his body betrayed his words and restrained actions. Kolt wanted her but wouldn't make a move to take things further until she gave him the okay, and tonight, she was more than ready.

Taking a deep breath in, her nervousness rising, she wrapped the towel around her body and opened the bathroom door, crossing the hall to Kolt's room. Her steps halted in the doorway as she took in the lean, powerful length of him standing by his bedroom window looking out over the farmyard. He was wearing a pair of cotton pajama pants and a t-shirt, his hair mussed up as usual without his signature cowboy hat. Looking relaxed and thoughtful, he turned, meeting her gaze, a slow smile curling his lips as his eyes locked on hers in a panty-melting stare. Everything about the look he gave her spelled out desire, and it took everything she had not to drop her towel right there and beg him to make love to her.

"I can slip out while you get dressed," he said huskily, walking towards the door.

"It's okay," she said, reaching for his arm. "You can stay."

KOLT SWALLOWED DOWN, his mouth suddenly dry, her words going straight to his groin. *God, I want her.* His eyes took in the swell of her breasts covered by the towel and the smoothness of her exposed legs. Walking over to the bed, she fished out a pair of panties from her bag and stepped into them, shimmying them up her legs, covering her most intimate parts. He leaned against the wall, unsure if he should watch but unable to look away as she reached for a sleeping shirt. Turning away from him, she dropped the towel, causing his breath to hitch as he took in the long creamy expanse of her bare back. He had seen her back bare like this before, had touched it, kissed it, feeling the soft skin under his fingertips and lips but something about her being this bold made him want to touch her again, slide his hands around her waist, up her supple stomach to cup her perfect breasts. The thought of feeling them in his hands made all the blood rush south, and an inadvertent growl rolled up his throat. Hearing him, she held the shirt to her front and glanced over her shoulder, giving him a coquettish smile. *She knows exactly what she's doing to me.* The realization hit him, and he met her darkening gaze. Without words, she told him that tonight they would not just be sleeping under the stars but making love.

She is ready. Ready to trust me fully, not only with her heart but with her body. When he planned this night for them, he had gone through every possible scenario and had tried to prepare himself for them all. He was more than willing to simply kiss and caress her as they fell asleep under the night sky. But knowing she wanted him as much as he wanted her and was now ready to take that step with him made his pulse quicken and mind swirl with everything he wanted to experience with her.

Slipping into her sleeping shirt, Jane pulled on a pair of pajama shorts and twisted her long damp hair into a messy bun at the top of her head before she turned to face him.

"Ready?" he asked, putting his hand out for her to take it.

"I'm ready." She replied, accepting his hand, her hazel eyes saying so much more than her words.

THEY PULLED onto the utility road, the clearing of the meadow coming into view, and MJ felt butterflies take flight in her belly. Kolt pulled the truck up just past the oak tree they sat under, giving them an unobstructed view of the burgeoning sky. The dusk had set in, the colors of a prairie sunset starting to fade on the horizon. Kolt made short work of setting up the bed of the truck, taking out quilts and pillows, making the bed of the truck look comfortable and inviting. He set up a portable lamp and pulled out a cooler he'd stocked with drinks and food. Lifting her onto the bed of the truck, she crawled to the end, resting against the pillows, and getting comfortable as he followed and settled beside her. Reaching into the cooler, he pulled out two lowball wine glasses and a bottle of white wine, holding it out to her. "Would you like a glass?" he asked, a flirtatious smile tugging at his lips.

Nodding, she watched as he poured them each a glass

of wine and pulled out a platter of crackers, grapes and fancy meats and cheeses.

"You really went all out for this," she said with a little giggle, taking in the spread. "I feel a little like I'm in a Hallmark movie. Girl meets handsome cowboy; cowboy woos her, and she falls in love."

Kolt's head swiveled with her words, his eyes capturing hers in the dimming light. "Did you say love?"

"I did," she replied, not skipping a beat as she reached out, smoothing her hand over his stubbled chin. "I am helplessly, hopelessly in love with you, Kolt Donahue."

A huge smile curled his lips up and his eyes flashed with approval as he looked around them, lifting the platter and quickly putting it back in the cooler.

"What are you doing?" she giggled as he threw back the glass of wine and gestured for her to do the same. She followed suit by downing it and handing the glass to him to tuck away, confusion and pure amusement on her face.

"I need two hands to show you how I feel," he finally answered, pulling her onto his lap, her legs straddling him. He cupped her face, caressing his thumbs over her cheeks, his eyes intense with lust and love for her. "I love you, Jane. With my entire heart and soul and tonight I want nothing more than to love you with my body, but only if you're ready. Are you ready, Jane?" he asked, inhaling deeply, as their foreheads touched, and eyes locked in a lustful stare.

"I'm ready, Kolt. I want you to make love to me right here under the stars." She whispered as they breathed in the same air, and her heart pounded wildly against her chest. With her words, he captured her lips in a deep sensual kiss that made her toes curl. Teasing her lips to open, she invited him in, their tongues sliding together in a familiar dance that opened the floodgates of passion between them. Her hips instinctively rocking over him, she could feel his arousal quake against the heat of her pulsing core. Unspeakably aroused and breathless, she pulled away and reached for her sleeping shirt, peeling it over her head and exposing herself to his wanton gaze. Her eyes met his, dark with desire as he looked his fill, before pulling his shirt over his head, revealing his long, lean, muscular torso, all sexy hard edges, and grooves. She wanted nothing more than to explore every hard angle with her lips and tongue, but as that thought entered her mind, he lifted her higher on his lap, cupping a breast and taking a stiff peak into his mouth, teasing it with his tongue, then sucking it deep making her cry out in plea-sure. Her hands tangled in his hair, pressing him to take more as her hips rocked over the hard length of him behind his thin pajama pants. Letting one breast go with a pop, he took in the other, giving it equal attention to the first, making her throw back her head and moan loudly into the night sky.

THE SOUNDS SHE WAS MAKING, needy, wanton almost feral, made him harder than he could ever remember being. Everything about her made him so ridiculously aroused he felt like a horny teenager, almost frantic to look at, touch, and taste her all at once. He needed to slow down, take his time, but Jane rocking over his needy erection was almost too much. Having thought of this moment countless times over the weeks they had been dating, he didn't want this moment to be anticlimactic for her, so he flipped her onto her back, making her whimper as he settled into the apex of her body. Unabashedly, she pressed her hips up into him, letting his hard ridge create friction where she needed it.

"Slow down, Pretty Girl," he breathed out against her lips. "We don't need to rush. We have all night. There are so many things I want to do to make you feel good."

"I want to do the same for you. But don't worry about me, okay. I have never…" she started. Pulling his lips from hers, he caged her and cupped her face, his brows furrowing as he waited for her to continue. "It's just, I've never been able to have an orgasm." She confessed, looking away for a moment, feeling the heat rise and settle in her cheeks.

"Oh," he said, his eyes flashing with confidence as he pressed his hips into hers. "Are you presenting me with a challenge?

She smiled, taking in his cocky smile and raised an eyebrow at him as she reached between them and slid her palm over the impressive ridge tenting his pants. "I might be."

A deep rumbly growl escaped his lips as he pressed his length against her before he raised himself to his knees and asked, "Do you trust me?"

REVERENT. That's how Kolt felt looking at Jane. Laid out before him, a feast for his eyes, with each dip and swell of her gorgeous body and as much as he wanted to taste her sweet soft skin all he could do was look at her, catalogue every part so he could remember this moment forever.

"I do trust you, Kolt," she answered breathlessly.

Sharing with him that she had never experienced an orgasm, he couldn't help but haughtily think, *well then let me give you your first.* But before he did, he wanted her drunk with lust, and he knew exactly how to do it.

Climbing over her, he pressed the edges of his body over hers, tracing the curve of her earlobe with his tongue before he grazed his teeth over the tender flesh and sucked at it lightly.

"That feels so good," she moaned out softly as his lips roamed. Trailing kisses down the column of her neck, he kissed along her collarbone, making sure to trace the line of each shoulder before he met in the middle and placed kisses down between her breasts. His tongue traced the circumference of a nipple, toying with the pebbled peak, then taking it into his mouth and sucking as his tongue traced circles around the tip. Her back bowed off the bed of the truck, and she panted, eyes fluttering closed, completely lost in sensation. Seeing her like this, so completely absorbed by his attention, made him want to give her more. To make her come completely undone. With a clear mission, he kissed down her stomach, her muscles twitching under his lips, so responsive to even the smallest of touches as he neared her apex, and the intoxicating sweet scent of her desire made him salivate for a taste. Rising back to his knees, his eyes met hers as he hooked his fingers in the waistband of her sleep shorts and underwear and dragged them down her smooth legs. Unabashedly naked, her legs fell open, and he caressed light circles on the tender skin of her inner thigh, his mouth pooling as he took in her pink center, ripe and glistening with her arousal. Dipping his head to her core, he inhaled deeply as he planted a solitary kiss at her apex just above the pulsing bundle of nerves, making her shudder in response. Jane lifted on her elbows, her eyes hazy with desire and brows knit together with uncertainty as she flashed him an apprehensive look.

"I have never had anyone go down on me," she confessed huskily.

"I promise it will feel so good," he said, his voice low and sexy as he licked his lips, almost tasting her already.

She met his hungry gaze, her apprehension diminishing as she replied on a trembling breath, "Okay."

With that, he lowered his head again and slid his tongue along her seam in one long, languid lick.

"Oh, God!" Jane gasped, nearly bucking off the bed of the truck and clamping his head between her thighs.

Hooking his hands around her legs, keeping them open wide, he lapped at her silky folds, taking pleasure in each unbridled rock of her hips, cry of sheer pleasure and drop of sweet arousal on his tongue. Circling where she pulsed until she was vibrating, writhing, and moaning loudly, he was sure she was close. The realization that he was about to give her her very first orgasm, something only they shared, fueled him. Knowing she was hovering on the edge, he took her sweet bundle between his lips and sucked. She cried out, her core pulsating as a flood of sweetness coated his tongue. Her gasps of pleasure, her loss of control, her exquisite taste put him into sensory overload and made him throb to be inside her. Despite his own desire, he continued to lap at her until she stilled and let out a long, drawn-out, thoroughly satisfied exhale.

* * *

OH MY GOD. *That's what all the fuss is about!* With closed eyes, MJ tried to swallow, but her throat was dry, and she was sure if she tried to speak her voice would crack and shatter into a million pieces. Her body tingled all over from the pleasure he gave her as she felt the heat of his body crawl up her and settle around her head. Opening her eyes slowly, Kolt was looking down at her, his brown orbs twinkling with pride as one side of his lips quirked up in a cocky, handsome grin. Heat rose to her cheeks, and she brought her hands to her face, almost embarrassed by her utter loss of control.

"Don't hide from me, Pretty Girl. I believe I just gave you your first orgasm." He stated, the slow, rich rumble of his voice husky.

With his words, she let her hands fall to the side and she started to giggle, seriously giggle, Kolt joining in and partaking in her amusement, his body shaking above her. "You are so gorgeous when you laugh," he said, brushing her hair from her face and framing it with his large hands, staring down at her. "And that smile..." his voice trailed off as he kissed her tender and sweet. She could taste herself on his lips, and the erotic thought of that caused her core to clench, begging to be filled.

"Make love to me," she breathed out against his lips. "I need to feel you inside me." His eyes darkened with desire as, at her request, he rose to his feet, hooking his thumbs into the side of his sleeping pants and briefs and sliding them down and off. Her eyes followed the movement as he towered over her, and his erection sprang free. Her eyes widened, taking in his long, thick length of him and her core pulsated with approval. *He is more breathtaking than I imagined.* Kolt dropped back down to his knees, his eyes shadowed with pure lust as he reached behind a pillow and produced a condom. She flashed him an amused look, meeting his wanton gaze.

"Were you expecting to get lucky tonight?" She asked, her eyes roaming down to his steel length and back up to his fervent gaze and sexy smile as he replied.

"More like hoping."

* * *

WITH EYES NEVER LEAVING HERS, he ripped open the condom with his teeth and made short work of sheathing himself, then crawled back over her body, nestling between her legs. He met her gaze and searched her eyes, trying to read her expression, which teetered on apprehension. Caressing her cheeks with his thumbs he said, "I understand if you aren't ready, Jane."

"No, no, I want this; it's just ... I'm a little scared it won't feel good. It has never felt good to me before."

Kolt's eyes softened with her confession, and he leaned down, kissing her gently, whispering against her lips, "Close your eyes."

She did as he asked, and he tilted her head back, dipping his tongue into the hollow of her neck. The move was so small, but the effect made a needy moan escape her throat and her hips rise up to meet his. He was right there, his thick cock pressing her entrance as he took her earlobe into his mouth and nibbled lightly, sending a shockwave through her body, and opening her more to him. Pressing forward slowly, her warm tight body invited him in, inch by inch.

"Oh!" she exclaimed as he entered her body slowly, caressing her neck with feathery kisses and tracing the line of her collarbone with his tongue.

Once he was fully seated inside her, he lifted his head, meeting her eyes, so much reverence in his gaze as he asked. "Are you okay, Pretty Girl?"

"Yes," she replied through shuddered breaths. "It's never felt like this. It's so full. So good."

He slowly pulled back almost all the way out and eased back in with a gentle thrust, feeling her body ease under him. "That's it, Jane. Just feel. Feel me deep inside you."

THE NEW SENSATIONS, the impossibly full feeling and his dirty words seemed to stimulate an untapped arousal within her. "Keep talking." She panted as he moved in and out of her with long, deep strokes that seemed to reach a place that was untouched.

"You feel so tight, so warm and so incredible around me," he said, his voice husky and wanton. His hips rolled and pressed with each slow thrust as the sinewy muscles of his arms flexed under her fingertips. The power of his body on top of her, claiming her, loving her in a way that was raw and carnal, was way more than she had fantasized about, and she felt lost in a world of untapped desire and sensation. Feeling the now familiar slow burn of her orgasm low in her belly, she met his gaze, half-lidded and lost in the throes of his own pleasure. She lifted her legs higher to deepen the angle and cried out when he hit a spot that ricocheted a surge of desire through her entire body. She gasped, her body close, so painfully close to letting go. Never had this felt so good, so perfect, so right. His body playing hers like a fiddle, knowing how to hit each note. "That's it, Pretty Girl," he cooed as he quickened his pace, the sweet friction bringing her to the edge. With one more powerful thrust, she shattered, her world as she knew it, forever changed as her body surrendered to magnificent pleasure. Wave after wave of sensation rolled through her, and she thought she was going to cry from the sheer satiated bliss of it all. She felt his body go rigid, and she opened her eyes to meet his, glazed over in pleasure as he stilled his movement, and she witnessed the exact moment he followed her there over the cliff and to the crashing waves below.

THEY LAY TOGETHER, a tangle of limbs and satiation. With no words passing between them, just a contented silence as Jane rested her head on his shoulder and traced circles through the smattering of soft curls of hair on his chest. Kolt was not sure he had the right words to describe how he felt right now; the only words floating through his mind were, *I love her.* She had chosen him tonight, trusted him, given him all of her, and never had he felt so completely connected to one person. Like their souls were cosmically meant for each other. Reaching over to turn off the portable lamp, he pulled the thick quilt up, covering their naked bodies as darkness surrounded them. Looking up at a sea of stars twinkling above where they lay, Jane sighed, planting a kiss on his chest and wrapping herself tighter around his body. "I can't think of a more perfect night." She said as she glanced up, meeting his gaze, her hazel eyes shimmering in the moonlight. He lowered his lips to hers, relishing the feel as the words of a poem he had read recently drifted into his mind, and he recited it to her:

"Each scar a star, a tale untold,

In constellations of stories bold,

In darkness woven, a soul's design,

Galaxies of emotions intertwined."

Kolt quoted as he kissed her head.

"Did you just make that up?" Jane asked, curiously lifting her head to search his eyes.

"I read it recently," he said, giving her his endearing lopsided grin. "It made me think of you," he added. "I know you have so many things you haven't told me, probably things you never will. I honestly don't expect you to. But know I love you, scars and all. Just as you, right now, Jane. And maybe someday the stars you see at night will no longer feel like scars, but promises for the future. Our future, perhaps."

"Perhaps?" she questioned.

"If you want a future with me, that is," he replied. "No pressure, no rush. I just want you to know that when I think of us, I think of forever."

Moving to her knees, she climbed over his hips to straddle him with her auburn hair, a ring of smoldering fire behind the light of the moon. "I think I would like to spend forever with you." she said, leaning in to kiss him, the softness of her lips a promise as the passion between them rose and they connected, making love slowly, gently under a sea of promises.

CHAPTER 9

MJ patted Prairie as she poured feed into his bucket. He snorted happily, digging his muzzle into the bucket, the sound of his teeth grinding the feed a joyful one. She scratched his neck, his muscles twitching as he raised his head and turned to her, catching her eye. "What do you think, Prairie? Do you think we should stay here in Primrose?"

Prairie whinnied, and MJ let out a happy giggle as she patted his back and exited the box stall. Ben was standing opposite, hay in his hand and a huge smile on his face.

"Sorry, did I just overhear that you and Prairie are staying here in Primrose?" he asked, his eyes wrinkling in that wise, endearing way they did when he smiled.

"Yeah!" she replied enthusiastically. "I really like Primrose, and if you're okay with me keeping Prairie here for a while longer, I think we're going to settle here."

"Stay as long as you want," he replied. "Honestly, the extra help you have given me has more than paid for his board, and I appreciate it."

MJ smiled as she picked up a barn kitten and patted its fur, holding it close to her chest. "Primrose is a pretty special place."

"That it is." Ben replied, meeting her gaze. "And you and Kolt are going strong?"

"We are." she replied simply, her face blooming in a blush thinking about their night under the stars.

"Kolt is a good man, and I can see how much he cares for you." Ben said, offering her a smile, then turning serious. "But if he ever gets out of line, you know I can straighten him out." Ben deadpanned, pointing a finger to his chest. "Me."

MJ let out a burst of laughter at his attempt at humor. Ben may be a giant in stature, but he was as sweet and gentle as the kitten she held in her hands. All joking aside, it felt good to know he was looking out for her and would have her back if she needed him. Like a big brother or perhaps even a father would.

The ringtone of her phone sounded from her back pocket, so she set the kitten down and quickly retrieved it, hitting the accept button and holding it to her ear, still giggling from Ben's joke as she answered, "Hello."

A low, dark, familiar voice answered, a voice that had haunted her dreams, and her stomach fell crashing to the floor. "Hello Mary Jane."

* * *

"Jane, Pretty Girl, wake up." Kolt's soothing deep voice broke through the dizzying haze. Her eyes fluttered open, blinking from the light coming through the picture window of the Prairie Sky farmhouse, making MJ close her eyes again.

"What happened?" she asked, squinting, and trying to regain focus as her head throbbed painfully. "Ouch," she groaned instinctively, pressing a tender spot on her head.

"You passed out." Ben replied, hovering over the couch like a tall oak tree, a concerned look on his usually composed face.

"Ben carried you inside and called Kolt," Ever said, sitting on the coffee table, a glass of water in her hands. "Here, sit up carefully and drink this," she said, handing her the water.

MJ took the offered glass. The cold condensation on her hand made her shiver, and she took a sip, letting the cold liquid soothe her dry throat.

"Your phone didn't fare as well as you did," Ben said, handing her the phone, the screen cracked.

"What happened?" Kolt asked, his brows furrowed with the question. "Ben said you two were doing the chores, chatting and laughing, and then you answered a phone call and passed out."

"I caught you before you fell to the concrete, but you bumped your head hard on my arm. Sorry about that." Ben explained, his brows furrowed and eyes downcast.

Ever stood up and rubbed Ben's arm in reassurance.

"Thank you, Ben." MJ said, looking up at the beast of a man with gratitude as she shook her head slowly, remembering the course of events. "I answered my phone and…" Chet's ominous voice echoed in her ear. The low, controlled timber that always made the hair on her arms stand on end. Alert as to where or when his hand may grab, or fist may fly.

MJ turned her gaze to Kolt and answered simply, "He called."

* * *

BEN, Ever, Hayden, Whitney, Kolt, Georgie and MJ gathered in the kitchen at Donahue Farm. Kolt's mother bustled around, pouring iced tea for everyone when the doorbell rang. She rushed to the door, and a tall man with dark wavy hair and piercing blue eyes entered in his Royal Canadian Mounted Police uniform.

"Hey, Cade." Mrs. Donahue greeted giving him a grateful look.

"Hi there, Mrs. Donahue," he replied with a warm smile, his eyes darting to the group around the table with curiosity as she led him into the kitchen, gesturing for him to take a seat at the head of the table.

"Thank you for coming on such short notice, Cade," Kolt said as he put his arm around MJ. "This is my girlfriend, Mary Jane Kasper, but just call her Jane."

"Hi, Jane," Cade said, meeting her gaze, his eyes reflecting kindness. "I'm Cade Isley, a friend of the Donahue's. I'm an RCMP officer at the St. Augustine detachment. Kolt explained your situation to me briefly. I hope you don't mind, but I have a few questions for you."

MJ nodded solemnly, looking down at her tightly clasped hands in her lap.

"We can leave if you want to talk to Cade candidly." Whitney said, rising from the table.

MJ glanced at her and vehemently shook her head. "No, it's okay," she answered, her eyes drifting over each and every person around the table. Each person that had become her friend and family during her time in Primrose. "I'm tired of hiding and so tired of keeping my past a secret." She said. "I'm Mary Jane Kasper, a domestic abuse survivor and I left my family farm in Smoky Lake, Alberta to flee my abuser, a man named Chet who I trusted, who said he loved me, then beat me and…" her voice broke with her words.

"You don't need to go on, Pretty Girl." Kolt said, putting his arm around her protectively, pulling her closer.

MJ's eyes flitted around the room, everyone's faces contorted with emotion and eyes glazed over with unshed tears. MJ just hung her head.

"You are so brave to share that." Georgie said, reaching over to squeeze her shoulder.

Cade nodded, meeting her gaze again. "You are very brave, Jane. So many victims choose to stay quiet and not seek retribution against their abuser, and there are things we can do to help protect you," he said with a reassuring smile. "We're going to do whatever the law will allow to ensure you're safe. Now let me tell you what we can do."

* * *

Kolt pulled Jane towards him, enrobing her in the warmth of his body, his fingertips feathering light touches up and down her arm. They had been lying here in his bed, in quiet contemplative silence for over an hour, neither wanting to recap the events of the day. After Cade had left, the rest of their family and friends had dispersed, leaving the two of them alone with their thoughts. Seeing Jane so vulnerable today, answering Cade's questions and being so open in front of everyone, the reality of what she was facing hit him hard. What happened today had the potential to completely change both of their lives. Either for the good or for the bad. The good being the justice that would be served against Chet when she pressed charges and his inability to legally see or try to contact Jane once she filed an Order of Protection. The bad being the mental repercussions of him calling her and reintroducing that fear into her life. Jane had come so far, and the last thing he wanted was for her to regress.

"I just don't understand why now. Why would he try to contact me now, months after I left him?" she asked, breaking the silence. "I know I probably should have changed my phone number. But what would make him decide to reach out after all this time?"

A conversation crossed Kolt's mind. A conversation from weeks ago at the rodeo. Thatcher Stevens from Smoky Lake, Alberta, had recognized Jane. *She looks so much like a girl a buddy of mine was dating back home.* Thatcher's words echoed in his ears, and his pulse quickened, fear pressing heavy on his chest as realization dawned on him. *I may have caused this. Fuck.*

"How large is the town you're from?" he asked pointedly.

"Smoky Lake?" she asked, curiously meeting his gaze. "I don't know about half the size of Primrose, I would guess. Why do you ask?"

"Do you know Thatcher Stevens?" he asked, internally wincing as he asked her the question.

"Stevens? I went to school with a girl named Cassidy Stevens, and her brother Thatch used to hang out with…" she stopped mid-sentence, her eyes widening and darting up to meet him. "How do you know Thatcher?"

"He's on the rodeo circuit with me, and he asked me about you at the rodeo in St. Augustine. He said you looked familiar." He confessed sheepishly. "He said you looked like someone from back home, and at the time I knew you were from Alberta, just not that you were from Smoky Lake."

Jane slowly blinked at him, and he could see her mind reeling with his confession, taking its time to fully absorb. Suddenly she peeled herself from his body and rose from the bed, her face losing color in the light of his bedside lamp as she paced at the foot of the bed, her brows furrowed as she questioned rapid fire. "Did you tell him my name? Did he ask you who I was to you?"

"All he said was you looked like a girl he knew from home named MJ and that you were dating a friend of his. He asked if you were my girl, and I said yes," he replied, running his hand through his hair.

"And this was after I told you my real name." She said, phrased as a statement rather than a question. "Shit!" she exclaimed, resuming her pacing and shaking her head. She stopped, and his breath caught as she turned to him, her eyes glazed over with a combination of anger and betrayal. "You knew he knew me, and you chose not to tell me about the conversation. A conversation that I should have been informed about."

Kolt felt his heart sink to the pit of his stomach and his throat tighten painfully. That was exactly what he'd done, and now he may have brought Chet right to her. Meeting her hurt-filled eyes, he spoke, trying to relay his reasoning. "I was scared you would run if I told you, and I didn't want to lose you. I already knew I loved you, Jane."

The anger in her eyes softened slightly with his confession, but there was still frustration and indignation in their depths. "If you had told me, I could have prepared myself. I could have changed my phone number, or I could have…"

"Disappeared on me," he added, putting his own words and fears into her sentence.

"I wouldn't have done that." She replied through gritted teeth, pure frustration on her face. "This place and you have become too important to me."

Striding over to her dresser, she reached for her truck keys.

"Where are you going?" he asked, scrambling from the bed, suddenly feeling panicked, the need to stop her overtaking him.

Jane held up her hand to stop him. "I just need some time alone to think, okay? I just need a little space to think this…" she said, pointing between them. "…and everything through."

"When can I see you again?" he asked, his brows knitting together with worry.

"I don't know. I just want to be alone right now," she said, reaching for the door.

A deep, cavernous ache formed in his chest as she left his room, and he heard her retreating footsteps on the staircase, followed by the closing of the front door and the low rumble of her truck starting. He hung his head, curling his fingers through his hair and pulling at the strands tightly. He felt gutted, and yet he knew the pain he felt in this moment was nothing compared to the betrayal she was feeling towards him right now. As much as he didn't want it, if space was what she needed, he was going to give it to her. Even if it completely tore him apart.

* * *

MJ SAT on the porch of the little cottage looking out at the expansive green lawn of the Hastings property. It was early morning, all quiet as she curled up in an Adirondack chair and sipped on her coffee. It was her day off, no Prairie Sky, no Hastings Hardware. Just her and her thoughts and perhaps a pleasure trip to the farm to go see Prairie. Maybe they would go for a ride.

Her mind drifted to Kolt as she took a long, deep sip from her coffee and let the bitterness of the liquid try to squash the bitterness she felt towards him right now. It had been three days since he had confessed to her his conversation with Thatcher, and she had left, letting her words hang between them, thick and heavy. She had walked out on him, not giving any sign as to when they would see each other again, and for that she honestly felt immeasurably guilty. The truth was, she saw his point, and it made sense why he had held back the conversation with Thatcher from her. As an outsider looking in, she was a flight risk, and the possibility of her running scared was a real one. The thing was, too many amazing things had happened to her since she had settled in Primrose. She had friends who were now more like family; she had two great jobs that she genuinely enjoyed; and Prairie was happy at Prairie Sky. Plus, she had fallen in love not only with the town but with a man who truly saw her and loved her just as she was. Broken, jagged pieces and all. She was in love with Kolt; there was no question. And he loved her, telling her not just in words, but with his actions. Kolt had more than proven himself worthy of her, and she needed to be okay with his transgression. Give him some grace. *So why am I having such a hard time getting past it?* She sighed and brought her coffee cup to her lips again, taking a sip and leaning back against the chair in thought.

"Hey there." Whitney's voice sounded as she walked towards the cottage with a coffee cup in her hand.

"Hey, Whitney." MJ replied, offering her a pensive smile.

"That doesn't look good," Whitney said, taking a seat next to her in a second Adirondack chair. "I thought I would come check on you. Couldn't help but notice you've been home the past few days and your hunky cowboy hasn't been coming around. Things okay with you two?"

MJ looked away, feeling tears prick her eyes. Whitney, noticing her emotion, reached out and took her hand, giving it a supportive squeeze. She turned back to meet Whitney's gaze, which was wary with concern, as she said. "I know, you've been through a lot in the past few days, and you must be scared that Chet is coming after you, but I want you to know that you are surrounded by an army of people that care about you and want to keep you safe. And your gorgeous cowboy there is leading the charge. Go easy on him. I'm sure that no matter what he did, he had your best interests at heart."

MJ knew he did, but could she trust him to be forthcoming in the future? And then there was the question of his trust in her.

"This whole time, we've been building a relationship based on trust, and the focus has been about whether I can trust him. Now it seems he never trusted me." she replied.

"How so?" Whitney asked, furrowing her brows.

"He held back some information from me as he thought I was going to run if I found out. And that information could be related to Chet contacting me," she explained.

Whitney nodded . "You know, you can't blame him in a way." Whitney said with a smile, meeting her gaze. "You must understand something about Kolt. He is a man who fiercely protects those he loves. And there is no question he loves you."

"I love him too." Jane responded with a faint smile. "But how do I reassure him that I'm not going to run? How do I prove to him that not only Primrose is my new home, but he is my home now too?"

"Fear makes people do things out of character sometimes or doesn't allow them to think things through the way they should. I think you need to give him grace on this and as for how do you prove to him that you're going to stay put? You enjoy your new life; you continue to love him with everything you've got, and you do what you can to protect yourself. Trust me, life is so much better when you're not running scared."

Whitney was right. There was a time for fear, but that time had come and gone. So, what if Chet knew where she was, and that she had moved on after leaving him? He was done controlling her life, and she was not the same woman that left that day. She was stronger, smarter and, like Whitney said, she had an army of new family and friends to look out for her. She had Kolt.

CHAPTER 10

*H*earing her truck followed by Prairie's recognizable whinny, Kolt knew that Jane was having a therapy session with Georgie. He itched to rise from his office desk and go meet her, wrap her in a hug and kiss those delectable lips. It had been five days since she had said she needed space, and he had obeyed her request. With all-consuming guilt wracking him that he hadn't been forthcoming about his conversation with Thatcher, he had lost sleep over the past few days. Despite this, he selfishly couldn't come to regret his decision, although he was beyond remorseful as to the outcome. He had set a target on Jane, all in the name of his own insecurities and fears.

I love her so much. The idea that she may leave Primrose and disappearing from his life was a fear that had consumed him from the moment they first kissed. That first bolt of electricity that ran through his body, when his soul imprinted on hers and he knew he was in love. He couldn't lose her, and he wouldn't lose her, not to his own selfish fears and certainly not to Chet.

Having spoken to Hayden, he knew Jane had filed for the protective order from Chet, and had pressed charges against him. His phone call, followed by subsequent threatening emails and texts that followed, were recovered by the RCMP from her broken phone, and a warrant was out for his arrest for uttering threats. Although he had done so much more to Jane than verbally abuse her, without photographs, medical reports, or witnesses as proof, they were unable to go after him for the physical abuse she had endured. Either way, Chet had the potential to be convicted and could be looking at five years minimum behind bars.

Where would they be in five years? He wondered. *Married, with children, a homestead of their own. Happy.* He knew he wanted all of that with Jane. The life. The future. There was no question that Jane was the one.

Hearing familiar laughter in the stables, he smiled, the sweet sound of Jane's giggle making his heart flutter. Jane and Georgie were back, and he glanced at his watch. *They weren't gone long.* Curiosity getting the better of him, he rose from his desk and exited the barn office, his eyes immediately zoning in on Jane. She wore curve-hugging blue jeans and his white T-shirt that said "Donahue Equine Therapy". He hadn't even noticed it was gone. *God, I love seeing her in my clothes.*

"You guys are back early?" he asked, his eyes locking on Jane.

"Yeah, there's a storm off in the distance, so we didn't want to get too far and get stuck in it." Georgie replied, glancing between them, trying to read the room. "We decided to reschedule our therapy session."

Kolt glanced out the back doorway to be met with a prairie sunset in full bloom with its vibrant colors dancing across the sky. Dark thunderheads sat rumbling in the distance but didn't obstruct the colorful sky glowing over the long grass and wildflowers of the pasture.

"Jane, can we talk?" he asked, turning to meet her gaze.

Jane looked to Georgie as she pulled the blanket from Prairie's back and reached for the brush. Georgie offered her a knowing smile and put out her hand, gesturing for her to hand over the brush. "You go talk with Kolt. I got Prairie for you." She said.

Jane gave Georgie a grateful smile, and her trepidatious eyes drifted over to Kolt, who stood patiently rocking in his boots and looking equally apprehensive. Walking over, he met her gaze, wariness in his baby browns, and put out his hand for her to take. Looking at it for a long moment, she hesitantly accepted it, lacing her fingers with his. They walked out of the far entrance of the barn, towards the west field, with the vibrant sunset colors as a backdrop. They were quiet as they walked; the only sound was the crunch of the long grass under their boots and the low, ominous rumble of thunder in the distance.

"I'm so sorry." Kolt apologized, breaking the silence between them, his head downcast. "I should have trusted you enough to tell you about my conversation with Thatcher. I should have trusted in us enough and our connection to know you wouldn't just up and leave me."

"Yeah, you should have." She replied, nudging his shoulder in a chiding yet playful tone. "Although I do understand your fear, and I appreciate you trying to protect me."

Kolt stopped, turning to face her, his eyes filled with regret as he said. "Good job protecting you. I may have brought Chet right to your doorstep."

"And if he does, he's going to be arrested." She answered, letting go of his hands and wrapping her arms around his waist. "I pressed charges and filed the Order of Protection this week."

"Hayden told me," he replied as his concerned eyes met hers and his brows furrowed. "Do you think he'll come looking for you?"

"I don't know, to be honest. Although I wouldn't put him past it." She replied with a long exhale.

"I won't let him get to you," Kolt vowed, cupping her face with his large hands, and searching her eyes. "I will never let him hurt you again. I need you to know I will do anything, and I mean anything, to keep you safe, Jane."

Giving him a knowing smile, her heart so full of love for the man before her. She had no question that Kolt would do anything to try to protect her. She buried her head in his chest and replied, "I know, RC."

The thunder rumbled, drawing ever closer, Mother Nature's warning, but they simply stood there, watching the remnants of colors change across the sky.

Jane looked up intently at him, her eyes twinkling in the fading light as she revealed her heart. "I remember when I was little, I would watch my grandparents and the way they looked at each other. Speaking without words.

They were so in sync with each other. Like they knew exactly what the other was thinking." She mused. "I always thought it was funny, and strange, but now I think it was the sweetest thing." Her eyes drifted back up to his, amber flecks shimmering in her hazel eyes as she added, "When you look at me, I feel like I can read your thoughts too."

His lips curled up into his handsome lopsided grin, mischief glinting in his eyes as he glanced down to her lips and asked, "What am I thinking right now?"

"That you want to desperately kiss me." she answered not skipping a beat, her breaths quickening with her words.

Kolt leaned down, their foreheads meeting, her fingers slipping through the loops of his jeans, bringing his hips flush with her body and his body responding to the proximity of hers. "You're right. I've missed touching you and kissing you this week. I've missed making love to you."

"I've missed you too," she replied, her eyes darkening with desire.

His large palm settled at the back of her head, tangling in the softness of her hair as he drew her mouth closer, brushing his lips to hers, gently at first, until their passion quelled, and their mouths opened, tongues finding each other in a delicious tangle. He tasted like a promise, a dream. Like the only one she wanted to kiss for the rest of her life. They kissed in that field, losing all sense of time and place as it started to rain.

The rain started out light and steady, quickly dampening their hair and their clothes but not dampening their desire as the rain pooled around their booted feet. An ominous thunderclap rolled, shaking the ground they stood on, the clouds now covering them in darkness, as fat raindrops fell from the sky. Startled, they broke their embrace, both surprised by how lost they were in each other, not noticing the extreme change in weather. Kolt looked up, blinking through the rain as the clouds took that moment to open completely and rain ambushed them in a downpour.

"We need to get out of this!" he shouted, the rain pelting their faces as he grabbed her hand, and they ran across the drenched field. Thunderheads rolled at their backs as the clouds moved faster, sending them in a high-speed chase with Mother Nature as they ran towards the shelter of the barn. Lightning cracked, illuminating the sky above them, followed in quick succession by a loud clap of thunder, causing them both to duck to the ground at the sheer magnitude of the sound. They glanced at each other, a combination of fear and unfurled desire in their eyes as they sprinted the remaining distance, reaching the barn and ducking inside. The barn was dark, Georgie having long gone into the house, and they were alone, wet, rumpled, muddy and ablaze with adrenaline and passion.

With heaving breaths, they panted against each other. Jane pressed against the wall of the barn by Kolt's body, both completely drenched by the rain. Carnal desire flashed in Kolt's eyes as his gaze drifted down to his white T-shirt, clinging to her breasts, her dark peaked nipples exposed through the thin fabric of the soaked shirt and cotton bra. His gaze lifted to meet her eyes dark with want as he caged her against the wall of the barn and a bright flash of lightning lit up the cased opening of the barn door followed thereafter by a deep roll of thunder just beyond the wall making them both jump and pull each other impossibly closer for protection. Jane inhaled his manly scent, and her lustful gaze lifted to meet his, dark with desire.

Pulling his shirt from her jeans, he lifted it over her head and pulled down a cup of her bra to reveal a pert breast, full and begging to be kissed. Lowering his head to her chest, his lips wrapped around her peak as he sucked her in, her back bowing off the barn wall and a stuttered moan escaping her lips. Moving to the other side, he pulled down the other cup and lavished her other breast with kisses, nibbles, and relentless sucks.

She cried out, "Kolt, I want you, I need you," as she fumbled with his belt, making short work of unbuckling him and peeling down his jeans. Reaching for where he ached for her, she gripped and stoked the steel length of him, making his hips roll into her grip, a feral growl of approval rumbling from his throat.

"Fuck, Jane, that feels so good," he said, throwing his head back and closing his eyes. "I need to feel you, Pretty Girl," he breathed out as he unbuttoned her jeans and reached inside, cupping the heat of her core with his palm, and sliding his fingers through her soft folds, finding her dripping with desire.

"Kolt, please." She panted out, sliding the jeans over her hips, taking her panties with them, as they both fumbled to free her from their boots and jeans. Once free, she captured him in a scorching kiss. Their tongues tangled in a sensual dance, and he lifted her, her legs wrapping around him, her wet heat teasing his body with its sweet softness as with wild eyes she begged, "Take me, please."

Positioning himself at her entrance, he braced her body against the barn wall, and lowered her onto him, taking her in one deep slide. She gasped as he filled her, the molten heat of her tight muscles clenching around him like a vice. Letting out a long exhale, he stilled, his eyes clouded with passion.

"Is everything okay?" she panted out against his ear, her voice husky with need.

"It's just so good, so fucking good," he groaned through gritted teeth.

Taking in his words, the look in her eyes turned wicked as she rolled her hips into him, deepening their connection. Another growl of approval escaped his throat as their mouths opened in a mutual moan, sharing each other's air. Thunder cracked outside, shaking the foundation of the barn, the horses, including Prairie, braying at the ominous sound. But they were lost. Lost in desire, pleasure, and the connection of their bodies. Setting a relentless pace, chasing their release like the storm chasing them across the field, a charge ricocheted through Jane's body as the lightning outside flashed, illuminating Kolt's handsome face.

"I love you," he panted, the need in his eyes intense and frantic. With his words, her body gave in, and she cried out his name, dropping her head to his shoulder as shudders of pleasure rolled through her body. Her inner muscles milked him with each wave that rippled through her core. With one last stuttering breath and press of his hips into her sweet heat. He came, giving her everything, all of him, every ounce of desire and love now a part of her. His mind, body, and soul were all hers for the taking, and although the storm inside her rivaled the one outside, she knew in that moment that she had chosen Kolt to be her shelter.

THEY LAY AGAINST HAY BALES, their clothes disheveled and damp, with blissful smiles on their faces. *This is what love is,* MJ thought as she lay nestled between Kolts long legs, his strong arms around her waist and the back of her head resting on his chest. "I love you, Kolt," she whispered in the darkness of the barn with the rhythm of the rain pattering on the concrete outside and the low rumble of thunder far in the distance. "I plan on staying here in Primrose," she said. Turning around to straddle his hips and cupping his face in her hands to meet his eyes, she added. "I love it here. I love this community. Everyone has been so generous and kind to me, and I can't imagine being anywhere else. Plus, you are here, and wherever you are, Kolt is where I want to be."

Kolt caressed her cheek, the love radiating in his gaze blinding in its purity. "I love you too, Pretty girl and I'm so happy you've decided to stay. I can't tell you how happy that makes me," he said, his voice cracking as he kissed her softly and pulled her into him for a hug.

Prairie Prestige whinnied in the background, and they both laughed.

"Seems Prairie is happy with your decision." Kolt

replied with a grin as he kissed her forehead and ran his fingers through her damp hair. They cuddled like that for a long time, listening to the rhythmic patter of the rain when Kolt broke their revelry by asking. "Have you given any more thought to showing Prairie? I mean, the season is well underway, and I know the Hanna Rodeo is in September and the town holds a horse show in conjunction with it. I'm competing that weekend, so why don't you join me and bring Prairie? I'm sure we can find the registration form on their website."

Hanna, Alberta. "I don't know." She said, shrinking back a little. "I haven't competed in years, and Prairie isn't ready. Plus, it's closer to Smoky Lake. I'm not sure with everything that has gone down with Chet this past week, if I should."

"If you don't feel safe, I completely understand. I can tell you that Ben was asking me about it the other day. Ben and Ever were thinking about taking a weekend away to attend, and Hayden was asking me about it too, saying if they can find a sitter for the boys, they were thinking of joining them. You would have lots of support around you and wouldn't be alone even when I am busy with my rodeo events," he shared. "It's completely your choice, though."

MJ thought about it for a moment. Ever since watching the horse show in St. Augustine, her desire to get back in the ring lingered. His offer was tempting. Plus, it was almost two months away, so chances were good that Chet would be arrested by then and, with any luck, be behind bars. Her eyes met Kolt's. "If I'm going to do this, I need new western wear, and oh goodness, I'm not sure where to begin."

A slow grin curled his lips as he replied, "I know a place in St. Augustine. We'll go shopping tomorrow."

* * *

MJ STARED at her reflection in the change room mirror, admiring the fitted western shirt she tried on, in deep navy, with intricate filigree patterns in rich brown and gold around the collar and the cuffs that made the shirt look like a work of art. It was beautiful but way fancier than the shirts she remembered wearing, and after a quick glance at the price tag, way more expensive too. The jeans she tried on hugged her curves to perfection and flared out at the end ever so slightly to make room for the most exquisite pair of navy and tan cowboy boots she had ever seen.

"How are you doing in there?" Kolt shouted.

"I don't know. It's beautiful, but…" she replied.

Kolt peeked around the curtain, slipping into the change room holding a tan Stetson that looked like the one gracing his head.

Turning to face him, his eyes widened, and she looked down at the gorgeous outfit, wrinkling her nose and feeling a little self-conscious.

"My God, Jane, you look incredible," he said, tossing the hat to the side and taking her hand to make her spin for him. Stopping her to face herself in the mirror, he took in her reflection over her shoulder and let out a little whistle, making a rosy blush rise to her cheeks. "How did

I get so lucky?" he said as he brushed her long hair aside, exposing the tender flesh of her neck as he lowered his lips to kiss and nip at her neck hungrily, making goosebumps form on her skin.

"Kolt." she breathed out, closing her eyes and leaning into him, her back molding into his front, the evidence of his arousal making itself known against the curve of her backside. "RC, we're in a changing room."

"I know, and we have a mirror too." he teased with a waggle of his brows, his teeth brushing the shell of her ear, his breath hot and heavy. "It would be kind of fun, don't you think?" he said, pressing his hardness into the swell of her behind, making her suck in a breath.

Turning in his arms, she grabbed the front of his T-shirt, bunching up the fabric and drawing him closer, connecting their lips in a passionate, smoldering kiss. Kolt had just slipped his tongue against hers when she pulled away, leaving him mid-kiss, his lips puckered, and eyes still closed. His eyes opened slowly to be met by her chiding yet amused smile. "You, sexy cowboy, need to get out of this change room before we get caught."

Feigning dejection, Kolt put up his hands, removing them from her waist and slowly backing away, slipping through the entrance of the change room but before he released the curtain, he gave her a coquettish wink.

Jane giggled and shook her head as she turned to face her reflection. Kolt was right. *I do look incredible.*

WATCHING Jane trot around the perimeter of the arena, Kolt leaned against the cased opening, arms folded over his broad chest. Georgie approached, offering him a quick smile as her attention went to Jane and Prairie.

"They're looking good." Georgie said, taking in the precision of his stride. "I have seen a bond between a horse and a human many times, but never have I seen the kind of bond and trust that Jane and Prairie have. He knows every cue of her body, every word; their souls are connected completely. It's something remarkable to watch."

"It is," he replied, a smile tugging at his lips. "Maybe I should be jealous, but look at them," he said, gesturing towards Jane, who had now slowed down to a walk and was leaning over Prairie's neck and talking to him.

He could see his sister analyzing him in his peripheral vision when she said, "I have never seen you like this, Kolt. Jane's the one, isn't she?"

"Without question." Kolt said with a melancholy smile.

Georgie's brows knit together, and she put her hand on his shoulder, seeing the glimmer of uneasiness in her brother's eyes. "What's wrong?"

Kolt looked down, kicking his toe in the dirt of the arena as he swallowed hard. "I'm so scared I won't be able to protect her from her past. They still haven't arrested Chet, and I know Jane was apprehensive about going back to Alberta for this show. Are we putting her in danger by doing this?" he asked, meeting his sister's gaze.

"Does Jane know?" she asked.

"Yes, I'm not making that mistake again," he said with a wince as he glanced over to Jane loping around the ring with Prairie. "She says she's done running and that she's choosing not to be scared anymore."

Georgie's mouth lifted into a broad smile. "Then trust that she has thought this through. Your girl is a very strong woman. Trust me, I know from our conversations that she's a very deep thinker, like you. I don't think she'd be doing it if she hadn't thought it through."

Kolt glanced at Jane, meeting her eyes from across the arena as a smile slowly crept up her lips. The smile that had him the first time, she freely offered it. A smile, she held back until she trusted him. A smile he had earned.

Georgie patted him on the shoulder as she added, meeting his eyes, "You need to trust Jane's instincts." Turning on her heel, Georgie walked away, her fading footsteps sounding on the concrete as she left the barn. *Georgie is right. Jane had thought this through, and if she felt safe, then everything would be okay.* Even though something in his gut said, *be vigilant.*

CHAPTER 11

They pulled into Hanna, Alberta, the modest town sign in the rearview mirror. Kolt leaned over, turning the music up, as "Someday" by Nickelback blasted through the speakers. He started shaking his shoulders to the hard-driving beat as he glanced over at MJ with a playful smile on his face. "When in Hanna," he said as he sang out the lyrics at the top of his lungs and gestured for her to join him. Obliging with a giggle, she shook out her long hair, not caring how bad her singing was, as she relished the freedom to be young, crazy and carefree. For the entire trip to Hanna, Kolt had done his best to keep the mood light and fun and when they passed the provincial border crossing into Alberta, he had pulled over to the side of the road and kissed her breathless until all thoughts of being so close to her hometown had gone. *Tricky.* Glancing over at her boyfriend, she couldn't help but appreciate his efforts. This trip had been fun, and even though she never thought she would return to

Alberta, she was happy she had decided to do this and spend this weekend with Kolt.

Pulling into a campground on the edge of town, a series of RVs, trailers and campers were already there, with men and women milling around in cowboy hats setting up their camps. Many had their significant others, spouses, and kids in tow. Sprinkled among the trailers were horses secured with cross ties that were anchored into the ground, allowing them to graze on the green grass between the trailers. Kolt backed into a space off from the other trucks and campers, giving them a little more privacy and overlooking a field, where the grass was uncut and tall. A perfect place for Stetson and Prairie to graze. Kolt leaned over, brushed his lips chastely to MJ's and reached up, caressing her cheek. "This is going to be a fun weekend. I'm so glad you're here with me."

"So am I," she replied, smoothing her hand over his stubbled chin. "I'm so excited."

"Me too," he replied with a wide smile. "Let's get the horses settled."

They both climbed out of the cab and made their way to the horse trailer, Stetson and Prairie obviously restless and wanting to be let out. These two horses had spent a lot of time together over the past few months, but traveling a long distance together in a trailer with confined space was a different story. Jane ran her hand over Prairie's back. "It's okay, sweet boy."

Kolt opened the back of the trailer, and MJ climbed in, hooking a lead rope to Prairie's halter and backing him out of the trailer, followed by Kolt doing the same with Stetson. Temporarily tying them to the side of the trailer, giving them slack so they could graze, MJ walked to the end of their campsite and surveyed the other trucks, trailers, and campers. The cowboy camp was a bustle of activity, and she smiled, taking it all in when her eyes settled on someone familiar. The one person here that connected her to her hometown, Thatcher Stevens. His campsite was across from theirs, and he tipped up his hat and offered her a nod, acknowledging he knew who she was, as he put his hand up in a two-finger wave. MJ raised her chin and gave him a nod in response, and he grinned.

Warm hands settled on her waist, Kolt looking over her shoulder to Thatcher.

"Are you okay?" he asked.

"Yeah. I can't run anymore." She replied, glancing up and meeting his concerned gaze. "Chet and Thatcher used to hang out a lot when we first met, but I'm not sure how close they are now. Smoky Lake is like Primrose. Everyone knows everyone, so it's not surprising that he recognizes me, and I can't assume he told Chet."

"I know. I just don't want you to be scared, you know?" he said, pulling her into him and kissing the top of her head with affection.

She turned, hooking her arms around his neck, and going on her tiptoes, she brushed her lips to his chastely. Cupping his face and staring deep into his wary eyes, she reassured him. "I'll be fine, Kolt. I promise."

Kolts eyes softened as he lifted her, her legs coming around his waist, his hands cupping her behind and giving it a squeeze as he cocked a curious eyebrow at her and asked, "Do you want to check out Betsy?"

"Betsy?" she asked with a giggle.

"Yeah, Betsy, the old truck camper," he said, gesturing to the truck camper that was fited onto the bed of his truck. "It's pretty nice inside," he said, waggling his eyebrows.

With a nod, Kolt set her back on her feet and took her hand, leading her towards the door. He dropped the tailgate and lifted her inside as he climbed in after her. Flicking on a light, she took in the interior. The confined space contained a tiny kitchenette on one side, a bar-size refrigerator and a tiny sink. A table for two with benches on either side sat across from the kitchen space, and there were two narrow steps in the middle leading up to the loft part that went over the top of the truck, the size of a regular double-size bed. Everything about the space was compact and cute.

"We can sleep up in the top part there, or if that makes you claustrophobic, we can turn this kitchen table into a bed too," he said, looking around proudly. "This trailer has been my home away from home for every rodeo since I started, but if it's too small or uncomfortable for you, the Hastings are staying at the lodge just in town. You are welcome to stay there too. I just prefer to stay close to the horses," he shared.

"Then, wherever you are staying is where I'll be staying." She said, looking around the small space. "It's kind of cozy, actually." MJ commented with a grin. "I like it."

"I like you in it," he said, taking a seat on one of the benches and reaching for her, to straddle his lap. Gripping her backside, he pulled her as close as he could, his lips a breath away from hers as he murmured. "I like having you here with me."

"No place I'd rather be," she said, bridging the distance between their lips and kissing him passionately. His body responded immediately to their sensual embrace. As they kissed, she could feel him growing hard between them as he pressed into her core. Pulling his lips away, he lifted her onto the tabletop, and nestled his body between her legs, looking up at her. She lifted off his cowboy hat, tossing it up to the loft and then running her fingers through the soft strands of his light brown hair, making it stand on end. His hands roamed over her jean-clad thighs, and up her sides, eyes locked on hers with a combination of love and pure unadulterated lust. The look he gave her made her feel like the most desired woman in the world. Not the shattered mess she was a mere five months ago, but a woman. A wholly wanted woman.

Her eyes not leaving his intense gaze, she reached for the bottom of her t-shirt, pulling it slowly from the waist of her jeans, freeing it and bringing it over her head, then off. Wearing a simple white lace bra, she leaned into him, his lips kissing the swell of her breasts, his tongue tracing the curves in a hot path, making desire pool between her legs.

"Kolt," she whimpered, as he sucked at her nipple through the thin lace, making it rise to a peak.

"Lay back." he growled, planting kisses down her stomach, the heat of his breath and lips on her skin making her ridiculously aroused. Doing as he asked, she lay back, her head resting on the hard surface, her hair spilling over the other side of the table as he reached for the button of her jeans. Popping the button and curling his fingers around the waistband to shimmy the jeans over her hips she brought her booted feet up to the table-top, and lifted her backside to help him as he slowly removed her boots and jeans, leaving hungry nibbles on her legs and thighs as he stripped her. Half-naked and exposed on the tabletop in just her bra and panties, he lifted her legs over his shoulders and pulled her to the edge of the table. Vulnerable in this position, with her legs spread wide, and only the thin lace of her underwear covering where she ached for his touch, she felt his hot breath at her center as he kissed the supple, tender skin of her inner thigh. The old part of her wanted to protest at this self-conscious position she was in, but instead she closed her eyes, deciding to put aside her insecurities and just feel. Kolt gently tugged the panel of her panties to the side and swept his tongue through her folds, making her shudder with pleasure.

THE FERAL SOUNDS she made were like putting gasoline on a fire that was already lit, his cock achingly hard and weeping as he feasted on her. He wanted to have her spill her arousal on his tongue, the taste of her something he now craved. Unabashedly, she rocked against his face and pulled at his hair, so much bolder than she was the first time he went down on her. In the past two months, he could see the sexual confidence grow in Jane and how she grew to trust him with her pleasure. She had become a woman who knew what she liked and was not afraid to ask for it. Coaxing her sweet release with his tongue, he teased and toyed with her sensitive folds as she writhed and moaned. So close to coming undone. His tongue rimmed her entrance and dipped inside, making her gasp and nearly bucked off the tabletop. Slipping a long finger inside her heat, her muscles clasped around it eagerly, and he added a second digit as he pumped steadily in and out of her. "Do you want to come?" he asked with a husky growl.

"Please," she cried out loudly, completely lost in her own pleasure.

Hooking his fingers, he found the tender spot inside her and massaged as he brought the bundle of nerves at her center between his lips and sucked gently. Chest heaving in a long breath, she let out a long-drawn-out moan as her body tightened and rippled across his fingers and he lapped up her sweet juices like a thirsty man. Bringing her down with tender licks and kisses to her sensitive flesh, the tension of her legs on his shoulders eased and she let out a satiated sigh, her breaths coming out in small staccato stutters.

Running his hands over her thighs, he kissed each side as she rose to her elbows, face flushed and meeting his eyes with a hazy, satisfied smile. "You are far too good at that," she breathed out as he helped her rise from the table to sit in front of him.

Offering up his sexiest lopsided grin, a hint of cockiness flashing in his eyes as he gripped the back of her head, drawing her down for a sensual kiss. Just as she tasted herself on his lips, a loud knock sounded at the door of the camper, and Jane jumped, a tiny squeak escaping her throat as she clung to Kolt.

"Donahue, when you're done getting frisky with your

girlfriend, come join us by the bonfire!" a deep gruff voice shouted from the other side of the door. "You are welcome to join us too, young lady."

"We'll be right there!" Kolt shouted back as he held back his amusement and met her eyes.

He could see the fire of embarrassment rise to her cheeks as a giggle let loose, making Kolt break out in a fit of laughter. "Do you think they heard everything?" she asked between contagious giggles.

"Oh, they probably heard enough." He replied, cupping her burning cheeks with the palms of his hands.

"Oh God." she replied, burying her face in his shoulder. Kolt rubbed her back and slid her to the side so he could exit the bench.

"Trust me when I say this, those old boys have probably heard or seen way worse," he said, leaning down to grab her discarded jeans from the trailer floor and handing them to her. Jane shimmied off the tabletop and took the jeans from him.

With his assistance, she made short work of redressing. They grabbed light jackets, and he helped her out of the trailer. Quickly checking on Stetson and Prairie, Kolt pulled two folding lawn chairs out of the backseat of the truck, and they made their way over to the middle campsite where everyone was gathered. An eclectic group of seasoned cowboys and rookies gathered roasting fat sausages on the fire, and a huge cast-iron pot of sweet baked beans bubbled over the flame.

"There's Donahue," an older cowboy said, with a brown cowboy hat, his skin lined and weathered, his eyes a light ocean blue. "And this must be your girl," he said, taking off his hat and flashing her a sly wink. "Find a place around the fire and we'll get you some grub."

* * *

MJ TOOK IN THE SCENE, like one you could imagine on a ranch or on one of those trail rides city folks paid to take to get the cowboy experience. Around the bonfire sat men who were tough and strong. Men who had been left bucked and bruised from broncos or nearly impaled by the horn of a bull. Men who ran on whiskey and adrenaline and loved every second of it. But what struck MJ the most as she surveyed the men, spouses and children around the fire was how normal they were. They weren't superheroes. Just regular men with wives, girlfriends and families. Regular men with bountiful will, wit and skill.

An older woman with greying dark hair and kind brown eyes touched her shoulder, handing her a bowl of food, and MJ accepted it with a grateful smile. Turning to Kolt, he already had a bowl and was shoveling a spoonful of the sausage and baked beans into his mouth. Pulling the spoon from his mouth, he chewed and gave her a quick wink, making her smile and shake her head. The strum of a guitar sounded, breaking up the chatter around the fire as a younger cowboy, not much older than MJ, started to sing. He serenaded them with songs from Johnny Cash, Kenny Rogers and George Jones as they ate their meal. Setting her bowl down on the ground, MJ heard the first few notes of the next song and immediately knew what he was about to play. "The Yellow Rose of Texas" filled the air as memories of listening to her grandfather's old record player that sat in their living room washed over her. The record player was large and rectangular, with intricate detailed molding on the front. It looked more like a piece of furniture than what it was, but the sound that it produced you couldn't get nowadays. They would sit for hours listening to his old records, with him sharing songs by Hank Williams, Charlie Pride, and his favorite, Gene Autry. It was a time when life was simple, and she felt loved. Suddenly she missed that old record player that still sat in the living room of her farmhouse, and, at that moment, she missed her grandparents. As if reading her mind, Kolt reached for her hand, interlacing his fingers with hers and giving it a light squeeze. She rose from her chair, and he watched with wariness in his eyes as she curled up on his lap, resting her head on his shoulder, his fingers tracing the shell of her ear.

"Are you okay, Pretty Girl?" he whispered.

"I miss them. This song was one of my grandfather's favorites." She said, feeling hot, remorseful tears prick her eyes. She closed them, causing a single tear to roll down her cheek. Kolt brushed it away with his thumb and pulled her in tighter, shielding her from prying eyes as she quietly cried, overwhelmed with a wave of nostalgia and sweet memories.

THE NEXT DAY, they woke with a start as the first day of the rodeo was upon them. This was a three-day event starting with timed events like bull riding and barrel racing on day one, the roping events happening on day two and on the last day the 4-H livestock show and horse show.

Overnight, more trucks and trailers had rolled in, turning the campground into a full-blown cowboy village. The Hastings joined them at the campsite, where they enjoyed a fireside breakfast together. With Hayden and Whitney finding care for their boys for the weekend, they opted to bring little Blakely with them on this trip. Kolt had spent some time with the Hastings kids, however never with Jane and watching her scoop their little girl into her arms, nestle her on her lap and sing her a rhyme about a teddy bear, resulting in tickles and fits of giggles not just by Blakely but Jane, was mesmerizing. As he watched her, he couldn't help but let his mind wander to the future. The thought of her balancing their daughter on her knee, with bouncy blond waves and his chocolate brown eyes, was so vivid in his imagination. This is what he wanted. This is what he wanted with Jane.

He must have been transfixed on her for a long time as he felt a solid nudge to his elbow, and he turned to see Ben sitting next to him with an amused smile on his face. Ben simply gave him an acknowledging nod and grinned. Ben was never much for words, and yet there was an understanding there. *Am I that obvious?* His eyes floated over their friends around the fire. Ever, Whitney and Hayden were all watching him too, their knowing smiles wide. *I guess that answers my question.*

Catching Kolt's stare in her peripheral vision, Jane turned, meeting his eyes, and curled her lips into the biggest, brightest smile he had ever seen. That was the moment he knew. Come hell or high water, he was going to marry this girl.

* * *

"WELL, THAT WAS A FUN FIRST DAY." MJ said as she crawled into the loft, climbing over him to settle in on his side. "Are you ready for tomorrow?"

"Yeah, I mean, it's not my first rodeo." He replied with a confident wink.

She giggled, the sweet sound making his heart swell with happiness. Since breakfast his mind had been wandering, preoccupied with unanswered questions, and the important conversations he wanted to have with Jane. There was so much he wanted clarification on, but asking made him feel vulnerable, even with their declarations of love. *What did that mean for the future? Did she want all the things I wanted? The marriage, the family, the growing old together? Did she still believe in the lifetime love that I do? Or did her past relationship taint those dreams?* He needed to know.

"Jane, you know I love you, right?" he asked, feeling apprehensive but forcing himself to continue.

"I do, yes," she replied, confusion drawing her brows together.

"I know we've only been dating a few months, but I know what I want in the future, and when I think of the future, all I can see is you and I together," he confessed, their eyes meeting. "I guess I'm wondering if you see the same thing. I know you told me you once believed in a lifetime commitment, but do you still believe in it? Do you see yourself spending your life with me the way I see myself, spending my life with you?"

She turned on her side, and he mirrored her, their breaths mingling in the small space between them, as she asked, "Are you wondering if my past relationship has tarnished my perception of what I want in the future?"

"Yes," he replied. "Because I wouldn't blame you if it had. You've been through so much, and I would understand if you can't give me an answer yet. It's just, we've never really talked about where we're going."

Jane's expression was unreadable, the amber flecks in her eyes shimmering from the moonlight coming through the slit in the window curtains of the camper. Her face remained stoic, and his heart sank to his stomach. *You're moving too fast, Donahue. You're going to scare her off. Why would she want to think about settling down now, when her world is still so unsettled? Her wounds are still too fresh.* So many thoughts and doubts flew at him all at once, and her moment of contemplative silence became deafening. Jane finally blinked, as if waking from a trance, and shook her head. His heart instantly sank to the floor. Her mouth turned down a moment, and she sighed as she rose, climbing on top of him and straddling his hips.

She shone down on him, her long auburn hair cascading over her shoulders as she leaned in and kissed him softly, causing him to exhale, the breath he hadn't realized he'd been holding. Brushing the hair from his eyes, she cupped his cheeks as she looked down at him, love caressing his face tenderly as she replied, "Kolt, I saw what a happy, loving marriage looked like. My grandparents were married for 43 years when they passed, and every day. I saw the love they had for each other. No matter how many years passed, no matter the circumstances of the day, there was never a doubt to them or anyone else that they loved each other. Despite the bruises, broken bones, and scars that I've experienced, my dream of having what they had has only deepened. My grandparents had a deep, abiding, unconditional love, and when I look at you, all I see is that kind of love. A love that lasts a lifetime."

A love that lasts a lifetime. Kolt's heart sighed with relief as he repeated her words in his head, and a slow, happy grin tugged at his lips. "I guess that means you see a future with me too?"

"I do." She replied with conviction.

"And what does that look like for you?" he asked, running his hands over her hips and up her sides.

"Marriage, family, farm," she replied. "Not necessarily in that order, but yes, I want all three."

Marriage, family, farm. There was nothing he wanted more. He could give her that, and, more importantly, he could give her a lifetime of love like her grandparents shared.

"I love you so much, Jane," he said, a swell of emotion rising with his words, making his voice crack.

"I love you too, Kolt," she replied, leaning in and bridging the gap between their lips. Their embrace delicate and sweet, a sealed promise for a future together. As their desire quelled and they made love tenderly, reverently, there were no more questions to be asked. Because Jane belonged to him, and he unconditionally belonged to her.

Day two of the rodeo and Kolt was up early, letting Jane sleep a little longer as the sun came up over the horizon. He sat next to the trailer, watching Stetson and Prairie graze, enjoying the calm before the storm on a day that would be extremely hectic. The cowboy camp was starting to wake, some of the older cowboys already up for a while tending to their horses. Kolt stared off into the distance, thinking of his conversation with Jane last night and about their future. Her words echoing sweetly through his mind, the feel of her touch lingering on his skin. Smiling, he touched his lips, remembering their sealing kiss, promising him that they would be together forever. So lost in his thoughts of the beautiful woman that came into his life like the roll of thunderheads in the sky, he didn't hear the heavy footfalls of cowboy boots on the gravel approaching him.

"Hey Kolt," a low voice said, breaking him from his thoughts as he glanced to the side to see Thatcher Stevens.

Thatcher stood there holding two steaming coffee mugs, with his perpetual cocky smile on his face. Holding out a mug to Kolt, he gestured to the seat next to him, meant for Jane. Kolt gave him a nod, and he took a seat facing the horizon.

"Thanks for the coffee." Kolt said, offering him a cautious yet grateful smile.

"Where's MJ?" Thatcher asked, looking towards the camper.

Kolt straightened in his lawn chair, unsure if wanted to answer but curious why Thatcher had come over. "She's still sleeping."

He nodded, turning back to the emerging sunrise, silence falling between the two men until Thatcher spoke. "Did MJ tell you we know each other from Smoky Lake?"

"She did," he replied simply, taking a deep sip of the dark bitter liquid and letting it soothe the edge that he felt in Thatcher's presence. *Where was he going with this?*

"Yeah, Smoky Lake is a small place. Everyone knows everyone. Gossip floats around like the breeze off the North Saskatchewan River, and everyone knows your business." he added, then chuckled low and gruff as he brought his coffee cup to his lips and took a sip. "Who am I to tell you? You know how people talk in small towns."

"Where are you going with this, Thatcher?" Kolt asked pointedly, giving him a cautious side-eye.

Thatcher didn't seem fazed and simply continued. "MJ leaving has brought to light a lot of stories and rumors that have been long buried in our little town," he replied. "Dark secrets that may hurt that woman in that trailer of yours."

"What kind of secrets?" Kolt asked, turning to face him.

"Secrets surrounding the death of her grandparents," he replied, meeting Kolt's gaze.

Kolt's eyes widened, his heart beating quicker as he asked, "What about her grandparents?"

Thatcher looked down and let out a long exhale, bringing the mug to his lips and taking a quick sip before he spoke. "Rumor has it that Chet had something to do with their deaths. It was an accident, but Chet caused the accident."

"What?" Kolt asked, setting down the coffee mug and rising from the chair, his hands on his hips, and his head down.

"I'm not sure what MJ has all told you about Chet, but his father is well known and connected in Smoky Lake, and I heard he used those connections to cover it up? The truth that is." Thatcher said, then went on. "Chet and I used to hang out as teens, playing sports together, always in the same class, and part of the same social circle, so I remember when he met MJ. She was so young, the same age as my sister, and he knew exactly what to say and when to say it. He would brag about having the prettiest girl in town and how if he told her to jump from a bridge, she would do it. Chet always had a darkness and edge about him. He liked control in all things and had a brutal temper. Even as a kid, he had one. Several years ago, our friendship had started to dwindle. Honestly, I was so tired of the shit he spewed. He's a real arrogant and entitled son of a bitch. But I always had my eye on what was happening with him and MJ. I didn't like the way he treated her, and every time I saw them together, I always thought about my sister and what if she was with him instead of MJ? I would never let anyone treat her the way Chet treated MJ."

"Why didn't you say something?" Kolt asked curiously.

"I did. I confronted Chet several times, but he would get defensive and angry. You didn't want to see Chet angry," Thatcher replied.

"He beat her, you know that, right?" Kolt asked.

Thatcher winced and ran his hand through his hair. "I suspected." He said, shaking his head. "Again, it's a small town. One person sees a bruise or a black eye, and the rumor mill erupts. Chet did keep her isolated as much as he could, though, so unless you were really looking, you may have never noticed it."

"Fuck," Kolt said under his breath, pacing back and forth in front of Thatcher. "What am I going to say to Jane about this?"

"I don't know. But I would be cautious of Chet. Word is, he's been a bit unhinged since MJ left him, and if the rumors are correct that he had something to do with her grandparents' deaths, I wouldn't put it past him to try to do something to MJ."

"Do you think he's coming after her or knows where she is?" Kolt asked.

"No, I mean I haven't said anything," Thatcher answered, holding up his hands. "I would never either. Personally, I'm happy she got away from him. She's always been a sweet girl and deserves so much better."

Kolt let out an exhale as the trailer door opened and Jane peeked out, offering him her gorgeous smile as her gaze drifted to Thatcher and in an instant her smile vanished.

SEEING Kolt with Thatcher this morning had put Jane on edge. Although they had exchanged cordial hellos after she appeared on the scene, Thatcher kept his greetings quick and excused himself, leaving her and Kolt alone. Kolt had told her briefly what their conversation was about and how Thatcher had assured him he had said nothing to Chet as to her whereabouts. And although she had chosen to believe Thatcher, something seemed off between her and Kolt today. Like he had been holding something back about his conversation with Thatcher. *But what did Thatcher say to make Kolt feel like he couldn't be completely forthright with me?* Whatever Kolt was holding back, she was sure it was to protect her.

MJ took her seat in the grandstand between Whitney and Ever just as they announced the name of the next cowboy competing in steer roping. They watched as the cowboy, whom MJ recognized from the bonfire, wrangled the steer and wrestled him to the ground. He got up from the dirt and dusted off his chaps, looking towards the scoreboard. 8.2 seconds. The crowd cheered.

"He leaned onto the legs of the steer. That made it harder to bring the steer to the ground." Ben said, looking up at the scoreboard.

"Next up, Thatcher Stevens from Smoky Lake, Alberta," the announcer said into the mic.

"Is that the guy from your hometown?" Ever asked.

MJ nodded.

Thatcher looked strong and in control of his horse as he waited in the chute for the gate to open, and when it did, he flew out of the chute, making quick work of flying off his horse and bringing the steer to the ground. The crowd glanced up at the scoreboard, 7.5 and the crowd erupted.

"Damn, that's a hard time to beat," Hayden said, leaning his elbows on his thighs. "If anyone can do it, it's Kolt, though."

Several other competitors attempted to beat Thatcher's time but fell short.

"And our last competitor, Kolt Donahue, from Primrose, Manitoba."

The crowd swelled with cheers, their group whooping and hollering, the loudest amongst them all. Kolt on Stetson, looked zoned in, focused, in complete control as they entered the chute. All queued up, the crowd waited with bated breath for the gate to open. MJ nibbled nervously on her bottom lip as both Whitney and Ever reached for her hands and gave them a squeeze. The gate opened, Kolt flying out with precision, dismounting Stetson and taking down the steer. Within seconds, he was back on his feet, grabbing his hat off the dirt ground of the ring and looking up to the board. Everyone's heads turned as 7.1 flashed on the screen and the arena exploded, Kolt taking first place. Kolt turned to the crowd, his eyes darting around to find MJ, and when he found her, he removed his hat, giving her a grandiose bow before he rushed to the railing and gestured her over, his eyes wild and gleaming with exhilaration. Phones went up and camera flashes went off around her, and a video camera from some local news cast was pointed towards her as she shuffled down the aisle and descended the stairs excitedly to reach her cowboy.

Reaching him, she said, "You won."

"I did," he replied, giving her his sexy lopsided grin. "I won the day I met you," he added as he took her face in his dusty hands and kissed her, his lips gentle yet passionate all at once. The crowd whooped and hollered around them, and when he broke their embrace, he flashed her a coy wink as he said. "I love you, Pretty Girl!" and planted another chaste kiss on her lips. Releasing her, he gave her a quick wink before he turned swaggering away, holding his hat up in the air as the crowd continued to cheer. While she watched him go, looking like every girl's cowboy fantasy brought to life. *I won the day I met you too.*

* * *

"WELL DONE TODAY, DONAHUE," one of the senior cowboys said as he clapped him on the back. "Are you and that pretty little filly of yours going to the dance tonight at the community center?"

"That's the plan." Kolt replied.

The cowboy gave him a nod as Jane appeared through the crowd, running towards him and jumping into his arms. Arms hooked around his neck and legs wrapped around his waist, he leaned in, connecting their foreheads.

"Hello," he said huskily.

"Hi," she replied breathlessly. "You were amazing today."

"I try," he replied with a waggle of his eyebrows as she tipped his hat up and sank his lips to her neck, giving it a little nibble and tickling the sensitive skin with his facial stubble.

"Kolt." she giggled as she slid down his body back to her feet.

"Are you ready to get all dolled up for the dance tonight?" he asked, wrapping his arms around her waist.

"I am. I just wanted to let you know that I'm going to head back to the hotel with Whitney and Ever to get dressed there. Should I meet you at the trailer or the community center?" she asked.

"Community center is fine. I can shower here in the change rooms and will meet you there." She nodded. "You better be ready to two-step the night away."

"You dance?" She asked, raising a brow.

"All true cowboys do or should! Two-step, square dance, line dance, I can even work with a good old polka if need be," he replied, with a cocky grin. "But I think my favorite will be slow dancing with my girl," he said, swaying his narrow hips and giving her a coquettish grin. She licked her lips and lifted her chin to him in invitation. Taking her cue, he leaned down, kissed her chaste and sweet, before pulling away. Jane turned, spotting Ben and Ever in the crowd.

"I got to go," she said, her fingers slipping from his as she gave him one last lingering look and turned to follow them.

* * *

MJ LOOKED in the mirror admiring her reflection.

"You look amazing." Ever said, putting the last pin in her hair.

"I can't wait to see Kolt's face when he sees you." Whitney added, handing her a pair of beaded dangly earrings.

MJ took the earrings, slipping them through her ears, and took another look in the mirror at the finishing touches. She had to admit she looked amazing. Like a young country starlet in her flutter sleeve thigh length pink lace dress. The neckline plunged low, showing the swell of her breasts and her long neck, fully exposed by the braided updo, compliments of Whitney. Her dark eyes were enhanced with a dusting of light makeup, and her lips were glossed in a shimmering rosy pink. Everything about it was simple and stunning and still felt like her.

"Thank you." MJ said, turning to the two women who had become more like sisters than just friends to her, and let out a long exhale, rubbing her hands together. "I'm not sure why, but I'm so nervous." She said with an incredulous giggle. "I feel a little like a princess going to a ball."

Ever and Whitney beamed at her as they did their finishing touches and the hotel room door opened, Hayden and Ben walking in, dressed in jeans, western shirts and cowboy hats, Hayden holding Blakely, dressed in a cute floral prairie dress with a jean jacket, her sunshine blonde hair pulled back in a ponytail. "Are you ladies almost ready to go?"

"Almost," MJ answered, taking a seat on the bed, and

pulling on her newly polished brown cowboy boots then rising with a smile. "Ready."

The community center was close to the hotel, so they opted to walk, as many others did, the entire community convening for this event. As they approached the hall, she spotted Kolt, wearing a pair of bootcut black jeans that hugged his muscular thighs, a white cotton button-down shirt, and his tan cowboy hat with matching boots. At his waist was the shiny new buckle for winning the steer wrestling competition that day. Part of her considered stopping and just watching him, standing there rocking back and forth in his boots with his thumbs in the front loops of his jeans. Everything about him said cool, confident, and endearingly boyish as he waited patiently for her to arrive.

GLANCING AT HIS WATCH, Kolt fielded smiles, greetings, and claps on the back from fellow cowboys and members of the community as he waited for MJ to arrive. His palms were sweaty, like a teenage boy waiting for his date for the prom to descend the stairs, and his pulse pounded in his head with anticipation. He surveyed the parking lot looking for Ben and Ever's truck or Hayden and Whitney's van, but no familiar vehicle appeared. Looking down, he rocked in his boots and hooked his thumbs in the loops of his jeans, trying to look cool and confident. A sweet voice called his name, and he glanced up to see Jane's auburn hair, her gorgeous smile and when the rest of her came into view his jaw slacked. She was a vision in delicate pink lace and her favorite brown cowboy boots. Their eyes met, and all words left his head as he took her in. Her hair was up in a crown of braids and tendrils pinned up showing off her long silky neck, her stunning dress plunging in the front, showing off the beauty of the curves the good Lord had blessed her with, and the hem of her dress hit the mid-thigh showing off her strong toned legs. He gulped down, his throat dry, taking in his angel decked out in leather and lace.

"Fancy meeting you here, cowboy." She said, cocking an eyebrow at him flirtatiously as her fingertips came up, smoothing down the collar of his white button-down shirt. "You clean up nicely."

"You're...wow...just wow." he managed, as his eyes, took in her lightly made-up face, highlighting her natural beauty and then boldly dipped down to her tantalizing cleavage that simply begged for his lips to trail hot kisses over. She must have seen the flash of desire in his eyes as she went on her tiptoes and whispered against his ear. "I'll let you strip it off me later." Kolt's eyes rolled back, and he let out a low whistle of approval, making her giggle.

Reaching for her hand, he laced his fingers through hers as they, along with their friends, shuffled into the hall. Long tables were set up around the perimeter, a bar was open at the far end, and the large dance floor was situated in the middle. A typical setup for a small-town dance. Country music played from a DJ booth set up in the corner.

"There's a table free over there." Ben said, pointing over the crowd towards a table in the back corner, his towering stature allowing him to spot it.

Making their way to the table, they claimed their seats, and Kolt leaned over the table announcing, "I got the first round." Taking everyone's drink orders, he turned to Jane asking, "What would you like to drink?"

"Whiskey and coke," she replied.

A look of surprise and appreciation washed over his face as he said. "Be right back."

Jane surveyed the room, taking in the cowboys with their families, several kids sliding and spinning on the dance floor, everyone clad in their best western outfits. Glancing around the room, her eyes fell on Thatcher, two tables down, and his eyes met hers. Lifting his drink up in the air, he gestured to her, and she gave him a hesitant smile. What had been niggling her earlier that morning came back, and before she knew it she was rising from their table and striding towards him, determined to get some answers.

As if he knew she was going to ask, he rose, excusing himself to his guests and rounded the table towards her. Her pulse pounding in her throat, he gestured over to the side towards a dark corner near their table.

"Hey," he greeted, speaking first. "I was hoping to talk to you."

Unsure of what to do with her hands, she put them on her waist, taking on a warrior pose, her body feeling the need to go into defense despite not knowing exactly why.

"Sorry, it was a little awkward talking to you this morning. Honestly, it shouldn't be considering we're from the same town and know each other," he said. "Kolt probably hasn't had a chance to talk to you yet about Chet and what I all told him this morning."

"It's been a busy day." She answered coolly. "But he did mention a few things this morning."

He nodded. "First of all, I want you to know I haven't told Chet you're here. Honestly, Chet and I haven't talked much in years, even though I see him in town from time to time."

"Good, I wondered about that," she added, rocking back and forth in her boots nervously. "I don't want him coming anywhere near me; that's why I filed an Order of Protection last month."

"Good, oh that's good, MJ," he replied, with genuine sincerity in his tone. "I'm not sure if you know this, but I passed the bar a few years ago, and I'm a lawyer in town. Needed a backup in case this rodeo thing doesn't pan out," he said with a wink before his brows furrowed and he let out a long exhale. "It sounds like you've done what you need to do to protect yourself."

"I hope so. Not sure if it's been served yet. At least not the last time I checked with the RCMP, but it's out there, and he would be breaking the law if he came near me." She replied, letting her shoulders ease, her mind registering that Thatcher was on her side.

Thatcher nodded, meeting her gaze. "What about your grandparents' farm?"

"I had no choice but to sacrifice it so I could get away." she replied, sadness and regret tightening her throat as she explained. "Chet assumed the mortgage after they passed, so honestly unless I can pay him out, he kind of owns it now."

"Isn't it your name on the land title?" he asked.

"Yes, I think so," she replied, starting to question all

that Chet told her. "When my grandparents passed away, I signed so many things. I honestly wasn't sure exactly what it all was, but their lawyer reassured me that I inherited the farm."

"Then whether or not Chet is paying the mortgage, you have your name on the title and have retained full rights to that farm so he can't take it away from you." he said as he reached into his pocket and pulled out his wallet. "I'll tell you what. Once things settle down more for you and you're ready to take back your farm, call me," he said, opening his wallet and pulling out a business card. "I'll do whatever I can to get you back what's yours."

MJ glanced down at the card, and back up to Thatcher, her eyes welling up with tears. "Thank you, Thatcher."

"You're welcome," he answered, flashing her a cocky smile. "It's nice to see you happy, and even though your boyfriend there keeps kicking my ass, Kolt's one of the good ones."

"Did I hear my name?" Kolt asked, walking up, holding their drinks. Noticing the card in her hand, he met her gaze and glanced between them curiously as he asked, "Are we good here?"

"Yeah!" MJ replied with a smile. "Just catching up with an old friend from back home."

Kolt nodded, the two men sharing a look of understanding before Thatcher excused himself and walked towards the bar.

KOLT TOOK a sip of his beer and draped his arm over the back of Jane's chair, his eyes constantly drifting over to the gorgeous woman next to him. Her hand rested on his thigh, and the simple heat of her touch made him want to throw her over his shoulder like a caveman and carry her all the way back to his trailer so he could peel her out of that pretty dress. Instead, he would settle for a dance with the girl he loved. Ben and Ever were already on the dance floor two stepping and MJ watched them with an amused grin on her face as big old Ben gracefully swung his wife around the dance floor. The music changed, and "Shivers" by Ed Sheeran wafted from the speakers, causing the dance floor to fill fast, with the song an unexpected favorite to line dance to.

"I wish I could do that." Jane said. "I have zero rhythm, and it always looks like so much fun."

"I can teach you." Kolt said with a raised eyebrow. "If you would like to learn?"

"You know how to do that?" she asked, pointing to the dance floor filled with line dancers.

Kolt flashed her his smile and rose from his chair, putting his hand out to her. "Join me on the floor and find out."

Jane's eyes flashed with delight as she took his lead and they walked to the dance floor. Kolt led her to the middle, the other dancers making room for them as he stepped to the side, crossed his feet, did a spin, and rolled his hips in time with the other dancers. Jane giggled in response as he came behind her and put his hands on her hips showing her the sequence again and this time shimmying his shoulders and jumping on one foot dragging her with him before pivoting and planting his feet to roll his hips against her backside Biting her lip in concentration, she followed, slowly picking up the tempo and before he knew it, she was rolling her hips in unison with everyone else on the floor. The look on her face was that of pure joy as they danced, and when the song ended and it switched to a slow, sultry country ballad, the dance floor became a sea of couples. Kolt pulled her in flush with his body as he curled their joined hands between their bodies, connecting their hearts and looking down to meet her loving gaze.

THE WAY KOLT looked at her, with his milk chocolate eyes, made her heart swell and knees feel weak. The love she saw in his eyes was pure and steadfast. The kind of love she had read about in all those romance novels. The kind of love that could move mountains. That could curl your toes and make your heart feel so full you were sure it was going to burst. The kind of love that makes you cry from sheer happiness. Tears pricked her eyes, and she rested her head on his chest, inhaling his familiar spicy cologne that gave her so much comfort. His large hand moved from the small of her back up to her neck, his fingertips lightly stroking the soft skin, making goosebumps form from his tender touch. Lifting her chin to meet his gaze, unshed tears mirroring her own, he lowered his head, brushing his lips sweetly to hers. A thousand kisses with Kolt would never be enough. She wanted a lifetime.

CHAPTER 13

Nervous was not even an accurate description for how MJ felt as she buttoned her western shirt and straightened her belt buckle in the long mirror on the wall of the tiny closet in their trailer. Reaching for her lipstick, she turned, leaning in to apply it. Taking in her reflection, she had to admit she looked the part. Like all the others she would be competing against in the ring. Insecurities crept to the edge of her brain, but she wasn't going to give them purchase. Not anymore. She had spent too many years feeling insecure and small. Feeling like she was worthless. Kolt made her feel worthy, and now, looking at her reflection, she saw a whole new woman. Someone cool and confident. A contender. Reaching for her cowboy hat, she could hear the voices outside her trailer, knowing everyone was waiting for her. Opening the trailer door, Kolt turned, his mouth slacking instantly as his eyes unabashedly roamed over her.

"Pick up your jaw, Donahue," Hayden said with a deep laugh.

"You look incredible," Whitney said, Ever echoing her sentiment. Ben just nodded his approval quietly, his blue eyes crinkling in the endearing way they did.

Kolt stepped forward, taking her hand as she stepped down and leaned against the shell of her ear, whispering, "Just when I thought you couldn't get any sexier. You Pretty Girl are a country goddess."

She felt the blush rise to her cheeks as he kissed her on the sensitive skin under her earlobe, making tingles prickle down her skin before releasing her.

"You have thirty minutes until your Western Pleasure Class," Ben said, glancing at a program.

"I'm going to ride around a bit and get Prairie warmed up." She said, letting out a long nervous exhale.

Kolt put a reassuring hand on her shoulder, and she smiled as she strode over to Prairie, who had been primped and preened, decked out in a saddle pad that matched her outfit and a perfectly polished western saddle. His ears perked up as she approached, and his teeth ground down on the bit of the bridle. Untying the reins, she spoke to him. "Hey sweet boy. Don't you look handsome!" she said, smoothing her hand down the length of his neck and curling her arms around him in a hug. He pressed into her as he always did, the affection between them honest and pure. Leaning into his ear, she whispered, "I know this is strange and we haven't done this in a while, but I want everyone to see how special you are today. Can you do that for me, Prairie?"

As if understanding, he let out a snort, and she giggled, rewarding him with a scratch between the ears. Mounting Prairie, she adjusted herself and positioned her reins, taking a deep breath as she sat proudly on her beloved horse and turned heading towards the practice ring.

* * *

KOLT WATCHED as Jane rode Prairie around a temporary ring set up for warmups, taking him through transitions from a walk to a jog to a trot. Prairie was smooth, following her cues with precision, and Kolt was mesmerized, taking it all in.

"A girl and her horse." Ben said, coming up beside him, with an almost proud paternal smile on his face. "They have something incredible, those two."

Kolt nodded, offering Ben and acknowledging smile and turning back to them. Jane and Prairie were extensions of each other. Giving each other strength both on horseback and in life. As he watched them, Kolt was unsure if one could exist without the other. Their bond was forged both by circumstance and destiny.

"I have never seen anything like it," Kolt added. "I think that horse would literally sacrifice his life for her and vice versa."

Ben nodded, a wistful smile tugging at his lips. "Is it strange that I feel like a proud father right now?" Ben asked, knitting his brows together. "Jane has become family to us, and I want you to know that if you break her heart, Donahue, you are in for a world of pain."

Kolt turned to his friend with nothing but amusement etched on his face. Looking up at Ben's deadpan face, the glint of mischief in his blue eyes gave him away. Ben nudged Kolt, knocking him off balance a little, and let out a big booming laugh before his face grew serious. "Seriously though. You'd better treat her right."

"I will." Kolt replied, clapping him on the back. "For the rest of my life."

The men shared a knowing nod as their eyes drifted back to Jane on horseback.

* * *

CLOSING HER EYES, MJ breathed in sharply and let it out slowly, trying to tamp down her nerves as she watched each of the competitors in her Western Pleasure Class enter the ring. Gripping the reins, she pressed into Prairie's side, cueing him to follow. Prairie was tense and resisted her cue.

"It's okay, sweet boy," she cooed, his ears perking with her words as she leaned down and patted his neck. "I know it's a little scary. I'm scared too. But you can do this. We can do this, boy. We're a team, you and I, always and forever."

Understanding, his tense muscles relaxed as he took her cue to walk into the ring. The judges stood in the middle, notebooks in hand as they directed them to walk around the perimeter, then jog and lope. Prairie transitioned with ease, showing his calm and cadence. They were asked to turn, going the other direction, and when they lined up all the competitors in the middle of the ring, asking each one to back their horse up, showing control, Prairie did it as she asked. Although the judges kept a poker face, she could see the judges eyeing them, pointing in their direction as they stood waiting with anticipation to hear the outcome. Jane glanced towards the stands where her group sat, and her eyes drifted over to Kolt, his hands resting on his thighs, back rigid with anxious anticipation, and as his gaze met hers, a slow smile curled his lips. *That smile.* The memory of the first time she saw his handsome smile, the day they met, flashed through her consciousness. How she was so guarded and refused to shake his hand. And how he backed away, giving her space. Looking down at her hands gripping the reins, she smiled, remembering how respectful and kind he was to her. That was five months ago.

Her life was so much richer now, and she looked up, her eyes drifting from Hayden to Whitney and over to Ben and Ever. *My friends. My family.* Generous and kind strangers who took a chance on her. Welcomed her with open arms, were patient with her even though she didn't have the courage to speak the truth yet. Her truth. They gave her a home; they made her family. She looked between them again, thinking about the time spent, conversations and laughter. Memories she would have for a lifetime. Each one of them slowly giving her back her life, in small and simple ways. Her gaze settled on Kolt. The man of her dreams. A man she thought she didn't deserve but who rescued her that night at that rest stop. He gave her a place to go, to be safe, to start over. He taught her to trust again. To want to live and no longer hide. He taught her what true unconditional love was. And gave her a reason to dream about the future. For all those things and more, she was immeasurably grateful.

The static of the announcer's microphone broke her from her reverie, and she gripped the reins firmly as she waited with bated breath. "We have the results, and we want to congratulate all the competitors that came out here today," the announcer started. "The winner of the Western Pleasure Open Class wins a trophy and $200."

There was a long pause, and her eyes darted to Kolt, his face anxious with anticipation.

"The winner of the Western Pleasure Class is Jane Kasper on Prairie Prestige."

Her family jumped to their feet, cheering loudly, as happy, disbelieving tears pricked her eyes. Jane blinked them back, but it was no use. They overflowed onto her cheeks, and she wiped at them awkwardly with the heel of her hand as she leaned down patting Prairie's neck exclaiming, "We did it boy!" Prairie strode confidently towards the award presenters, and the pride in Prairie's stance matched hers as they were handed the trophy and pictures were taken. Her beloved horse knew he had done well and had done it all for her.

* * *

"Jane!" Kolt shouted, jogging up to her near the outside doors of the area with Ben and Hayden following him.

Jane dismounted Prairie and walked over to him, a wide smile and her shiny new trophy in hand. Ben took Prairie's reins, and Jane walked into Kolt embrace, another wave of emotion threatening to spill out.

"I am so proud of you, Pretty Girl," he cooed, his arms encircling her in a hug.

"Don't forget him." Ben said in his deep baritone as he

patted Prairie and gave him a scratch on the neck. Prairie responded with a snort, making them all smile.

"When's your next class?" Hayden asked.

"Showmanship is on in about an hour." Jane replied. "I'm going to take Prairie back to the trailer, untack him and give him a quick brush down."

"Do you need my help?" Kolt asked.

"No, I'm good," she said, taking the reins from Ben.

"Okay, we'll be in the stands, ready to cheer you on." Kolt said, reaching over and caressing her cheek. "I love you," he breathed out as he tilted his hat up and brushed his lips gently to hers.

Pulling back, he smoothed his fingertips down her cheek, the feel of her skin like satin to his touch. Her long eyelashes fluttered with his caress as she replied breathlessly, "I love you too, Kolt, so very much."

With a full heart and one more chaste kiss, he watched her walk Prairie out of the arena towards their truck and trailer.

MJ STRODE TOWARDS THE TRAILER, needing this time alone to talk with her beloved horse. With one more class and the end of this incredible weekend ending soon, she needed to get her head around everything that had happened in a few short days. Her conversation about the future with Kolt, the discussion with Thatcher and now taking home first place from her first horse show in years, her head and heart felt full to bursting. She needed to talk to her best friend, and she knew Prairie would listen. Over the years she spent countless days and nights in his box stall or on rides, sharing stories about her day, as well as her deepest, darkest secrets and dreams with him. Every time Prairie would perk up his ears and take in each word like he was dying to hear what she had to say. Prairie had become her biggest confidante.

"What do you think, sweet boy?" she asked. "Kolts pretty special, isn't he? Prairie snorted, his ears high and open as they reached the trailer and she let go of his reins to unfasten the bridle, slipping it off him and hanging it on a hook on the side of the horse trailer. "I can see us getting married, having a family together…" she went on with a serene smile as she unbuckled the saddle and lifted it off, setting it on top of a portable saddle horse. Removing the saddle pad, she went on, "…I can see us building our farm in the meadow and see you in the pasture eating the long grass and wildflowers." She added as she reached for a brush and started brushing out his coat, back sweaty from the saddle and pad. "I can see us growing old together." The thought gave her heart a sense of peace and contentment she had always wanted. Pausing her brushing, she wrapped her arms around Prairie's neck as she said, "Oh Prairie, Kolt is the one."

"Hello Mary Jane." A dark, gruff voice sounded behind her. A voice she knew too well and hoped she would never hear again. *Chet.* "That's a pretty picture you painted there with your cowboy." *No, no, he can't be here.* Swallowing hard, her mouth instantly dry, she didn't need to turn around to know he had drawn closer. The hair on her arms stood up, and her pulse spiked as the awareness of danger and fear made her head swirl dizzyingly. He was standing so close now she could feel his hot breath against her ear as he went on. "Too bad you belong to me," he growled low and menacing, followed by a chiding tsk tsk. "I told you; you couldn't leave me, didn't I? I will always find you."

She felt something hard pressed into her side, and her breath caught as her eyes flitted down to the visible dark steel of a pistol pressed to her hip. She tried to swallow, but her mouth was too dry, and her skin grew clammy.

"Imagine my surprise when I turn on the local news to see my girlfriend, who disappeared months ago, kissing some fucking rodeo clown, right here in my backyard. Right here under my nose, just a few hours away," he said, grinding his teeth with his words. The sound made her cringe like fingernails on a chalkboard. "Do you remember what I said I would do if you left me?" he asked, hissing in her ear. Panic filled her chest, the memory too awful and the fear of that day the catalyst for her escape. "I told you I was going to kill that fucking horse of yours." Chet laughed maniacally in her ear as he leaned in further, his lips brushing her lobe as he whispered low and clear, "Just like I killed your Grandparents."

She wobbled slightly, her knees feeling weak, and her stomach clenched, bile rising to her throat with his confession as his words echoed in her head and finally registered. *He killed my grandparents.* His breath left her skin, and she could feel him take a step back. Turning, she met his sinister gaze, wild and unhinged.

"It was almost too easy. Just a few tweaks to their brakes and a freshly graveled road," he said with another unhinged laugh as he passed the gun between his hands slowly back and forth. Jane's eyes automatically tracked the movement as Chet went on. "Did you know your grandfather told me to stay away from you?" he asked. "I couldn't have him around, telling you to leave me. I couldn't just sit back and let him fill your mind with lies and tell you that I'm not good for you. That, I'm not worthy of his beloved MJ," he said, pointing the pistol at her. "I loved you," he said, coming closer and pressing her back into the trailer, his large imposing body making her head spin with fear and disgust, the pistol poised in his hand so close to her head. "Tell me you love me," he said, bringing his face within an inch of hers.

"No," she managed to squeak out defiantly.

His large hand came up under her chin, and he squeezed it hard, her teeth biting into her cheek painfully under his bruising touch. Anger flashed in Chet's eyes as he sucked in a breath between his teeth and demanded, "Tell me you're coming home with me."

A tiny shake of her head was all she could manage, her chest heaving, trying to take a full breath, under the suffocation of his heavy body pressed to hers.

Chet let go of her face and staggered back as if wounded by her words, the pistol still firm in his grip, his eyes now blazing with anger. Prairie whinnied behind him, bringing Chet's attention to her horse, whom she realized in that moment she hadn't tied up yet.

"Fucking horse," he said, turning his back to her and walking over to Prairie, cocking the gun at him as Prairie backed up. "I should just shoot you right now."

"No," Jane said, running at him and knocking his arm

away, causing a shot to fire, echoing through the parking lot.

"Fucking bitch," he said, twisting and hitting the side of her face with the hard handle of the gun. Blinding pain radiated through her temple as she stumbled backwards and hit her head against the metal side of the trailer, then slumped to the ground in a daze. "I will kill you too if you try that again," he warned, pointing the pistol at her before turning again to Prairie and cocking the gun at him.

Through the dizzy haze, everything became a blur, as she lay crumpled against the trailer, feeling the sharpness of pain on the side of her head, and the wet trickle of blood against the side of her face. Chet turned; Prairie reared up, another gunshot. Closing her eyes, she couldn't look as she squeaked out, "No." When her eyes opened, her vision cloudy with edges slowly fading, Chet was lying on the ground, unmoving, dark crimson framing his head, and her horse, her dearest friend, was standing over him tall and fierce before he fell to the ground with a loud thud. Voices, commotion, blurred faces around her and gasps of shock as familiar warm hands smoothed over her face cooing, "Pretty Girl stay with me". His baby browns were the last thing she saw as the darkness descended.

KOLT WAS STANDING outside the arena with Ben and Hayden when they were stopped by several of his rodeo friends all raving about Jane and Prairie Prestige. Suddenly a gunshot sounded, and Kolt's eyes turned to the parking lot across from the arena. The sound came from that direction. The direction of their trailer. The direction Jane had gone with Prairie.

"Holy shit, was that a gunshot?" Hayden asked with wide eyes looking in the direction of the trailer.

Jane and Prairie are back at the trailer. Kolt's stomach rolled as fear filled his chest and one name escaped his lips, "Chet." He knew, he knew at that moment, the woman he loved more than life itself and her beloved horse were in danger, and he took off running. Running across the parking lot towards the trailer and the echoing sound of the gunshot. With adrenaline pumping through his limbs, another shot fired, this time unmistakably coming from their trailer. A bloodcurdling scream, unsure if it was from man or beast, followed simultaneously by a loud thud as he rounded the truck. What he saw there, sent him into a state of shock, Prairie on the ground, his neck bleeding from a gunshot wound, Jane slumped against the trailer, limp and bleeding from her head and a hulking man lying close to her on his back, his head bashed in a pool of blood, its contents seeping through the cracks of his skull and his eyes wide and lifeless.

"I got Prairie!" Ben exclaimed, his usual calm demeanor wracked with fear. "You go to Jane."

Kolt rushed to her side, her long lashes fluttering shut, then opening to small slits as he dropped to his knees, surveying her with a fear that she had been shot and trying to find the source of the blood trickling down the side of her face. The source appeared to be a deep gash on her head, and internal relief washed through him as he took in her slowly swelling face. "Pretty Girl, I'm here, stay with me." he said, encouraging her to keep her eyes open as his voice broke.

Hayden had his phone out, calling 911 as a crowd started to gather with shrieks, gasps and whispers of "oh my god" sounding at the gruesome scene around them. Kolt glanced at Ben, who had taken off his shirt, trying to stop the blood that was seeping from Prairie's neck. Friends from the cowboy camp were bringing towels to try to help, one bringing a blanket to cover Chet's lifeless body, the pistol lying just inches from his hand. As Kolt continued to talk to Jane to keep her lucid until the paramedics arrived, it wasn't difficult to piece together what had happened there. Chet had threatened Jane, and Prairie saved her by trampling Chet and taking a bullet. A painful lump constricted Kolt's throat as he glanced at Prairie, their eyes meeting and something indescribable passing between them. With his earlier words to Ben playing back in his mind, *I think that horse would literally sacrifice his life for her.* "Prairie saved her life," he whispered. Jane's eyes slowly, hazily drifted to his as she managed to breathe out "Prairie" and went limp in his arms.

THE STEADY BEEP of heart monitors first broke MJ from her slumber. There was shuffling of feet, the low murmur of people whispering, their words unclear as she tried to open her eyes and make out where she was. *The hospital.* With heavy eyelids, she willed herself to open them. The familiar warm touch on her hand and the rich soothing timbre of Kolt's voice came through. "Please wake up, Pretty Girl." Her eyes slowly opened, adjusting to the light, everything blurry but slowly coming into focus. Kolt was at her bedside, his warm, melting chocolate eyes, red rimmed, and puffy. He had been crying. Kolt leaned down, kissing the back of her hand, and she squeezed her fingers into his palm as her parched lips parted and one name came out. "Prairie."

Another familiar voice sounded in the room, a deep baritone that had brought her a sense of calm so many times over the past months. *Ben.* "He's recovering at an animal hospital in Hanna," Ben said, stepping forward, his huge hulking body shielding her from the harsh hospital lights overhead. "He was shot, but the bullet just missed his spine and esophagus. He is expected to make a full recovery."

She blinked slowly, registering his words. *Prairie was shot.* A flashback of what happened ran through her mind suddenly like a film reel, each tiny moment unfolding and becoming clearer. A swell of emotion filled her chest painfully as she remembered what happened, the gunshot, her desperate plea as Prairie reared up, came down on Chet, taking the bullet and knocking Chet to the ground. She could hear Prairie's snorts, Chet's blood-curdling scream as Prairie mustered enough strength to rear up again and administer a second blow, this time to Chet's head. Hot, stinging tears pricked her eyes as realization of what Prairie had done hit her square in the chest. Prairie, whose life she saved on the day he was born, had repaid the favor by saving hers.

"Prairie saved my life." She managed through the flood of tears now cascading down her cheeks.

"He did." Kolt confirmed, rising to sit on the edge of her bed, his loving eyes shining with tears of his own. He swallowed down to try to steady his emotions as his large palm came up and rested gently on her stomach. "He saved both your life and our baby's life."

Jane blinked, taking in his words slowly, deliberately, her eyes growing wide and her hand instinctively coming over his. "Our baby?"

"When they brought you in, they had to do a lot of blood work and tests, one of which ruled out pregnancy and well, it came back positive." he answered with his endearing lopsided grin making her heart swell and fill with love.

"I'm going to give you a moment alone." Ben said, meeting her gaze, his smile making the sides of his eyes crinkle. "You have a waiting room full of family and friends who are waiting to hear that you're awake. Let me know when you're ready for some visitors." He finished giving her a wink.

Watching him walk to the door, she croaked out, "Ben". He turned, his eyes full of adoration and compassion. "Thank you."

Glancing down to steady his emotions, his Adam's apple bobbing with a strained swallow, he looked back up, meeting her gaze as he replied. "Anytime, kid." Then, he exited the room.

MJ's gaze drifted back to Kolt, tears in his eyes as they met hers, and he reached over carefully, wiping the tears from her cheeks. Although she could feel the pain of the bruises on her face and the painful tightness of the skin stitched together at her hairline, she leaned into his touch, letting the warmth of his hand comfort her as her eyes closed. Opening her eyes slowly, she let out a long-drawn-out exhale. A breath she felt like she had been holding since the day she left her home in Smoky Lake all those months ago. It was a cleansing breath. A breath that ended the dark and twisted chapter of her life with Chet and began a new one, bright and beautiful with Kolt. Opening her eyes, they met Kolt's, and she saw it. The life, the children, the farm. Everything she wanted for her future, in the depths of his loving gaze. With the past in the rear-view mirror, their future cresting on the horizon.

"You know what this baby means, right?" he said, glancing down at her stomach. "It means a new start and that we should probably get married."

"Are you proposing?" Jane asked with a wistful smile, her brows knit together. "Not exactly romantic, RC."

Kolt chuckled low and deep and laced his fingers with hers, rubbing his thumb over her ring finger. "Not yet, but I will be soon, and I plan on knocking your boots off with how romantic it will be."

"Oh, really?" she giggled.

"Damn straight." he said, leaning in, his forehead meeting hers, their eyes locked and their breaths mingling hot and heady. "Because you, Pretty Girl, deserve the world, and I will spend the rest of my life giving it to you."

And with that, he bridged the gap between their lips and kissed her tenderly. A sweet kiss to seal his promise of forever.

CHAPTER 14

The weather had grown cold, and a blanket of freshly fallen snow clung to the trees as sparkling hoarfrost. As soon as MJ had woken that morning and glanced out the window, with Kolt's steady snoring as her morning soundtrack, she felt the urge to go to the barn and saddle up Prairie. Riding in the snow was one of her favorite things, and she knew Prairie loved it too. She sighed, smoothing her hand over the small swell of her belly and smiled, understanding it was just as well. At 12 weeks pregnant and with Prairie eight weeks out from having been shot, she was aware she couldn't take the risk and needed to let her horse take it easy.

Thinking back to the day she was discharged from the hospital, bruised, and bandaged, all she wanted was to see Prairie. So, Kolt drove her to the animal hospital in Hanna, and when she saw him, she sobbed. His neck was wrapped up to cover the wound, and he was simply lying down in a box stall, looking so sad, weak, and helpless. Crouching down, she spoke to him, not caring that the vet and Kolt were listening. "Thank you, sweet boy," she said, wiping the tears from her cheeks. "You are my best friend and now my hero." His large black orbs softened with her words as he let out a weak whinny. "I love you too, my Prairie Prestige," she said, lying next to him, right there in his straw bed. Kolt stayed close but stepped away, giving them a moment alone.

Kolt had been there through it all. Holding her hand as Chet's father threatened to sue MJ if she didn't have Prairie put down for trampling his son, then dropping the charges as other victims came forward revealing Chet's sordid history of domestic violence, and the investigation into his involvement in the death of her grandparents was reopened. Last she heard, evidence was uncovered determining Chet was to blame for her grandparent's death, and he was laid to rest in a small private ceremony. A dark chapter of her life now closed.

Although it was difficult to return to her grandparents' farm, Kolt helped her pack up the record player along with the remainder of her memories she had left behind and, with Thatcher's guidance, the farm was put up for sale. When they returned to Primrose, Whitney and Ever helped her pack up her belongings, and Ben and Hayden moved everything she owned to the Donahue farm. She was sad to say goodbye to the cottage, but she knew that wherever Kolt was, was exactly where she wanted to be. Now her days were filled with Kolt, his family, horses and the anticipation and excitement surrounding her pregnancy. With a calming sense of peace finally settling over her life, MJ finally felt free. Free of her past, free of her fear, free to live the life she dreamed of with Kolt. There was only one thing left to do. Get engaged and marry the man she loved.

I wonder what he's waiting for? Perhaps Christmas? He did say he would make it romantic, and a holiday engagement would make it magical.

Familiar strong arms came around her waist, Kolt's large hands resting on her stomach, and she leaned back against his chest. She closed her eyes, breathing in his scent and absorbing the warmth of his touch. *This never gets old.*

"Good morning, Pretty Girl," Kolt said, nuzzling his thick morning stubble against the side of her face, making her squirm in his arms. "How's my girl and our little lime doing today?" He asked, smoothing his large palms over her tiny baby bump.

"Lime?" she questioned with a giggle as she turned, going on her tiptoes and looping her arms around his neck.

"Yeah, you're twelve weeks today, and Google says our baby is approximately the size of a lime," he replied, mirroring her laughter, and pulling her closer. "It got me thinking about baby names. Hmmm...what about Margarita or Tequila? Personally, I think Tequila Donahue has a nice ring to it."

MJ threw her head back with a laugh. "No way am I going to name this baby Tequila! Besides what makes you think it's a girl?"

He shrugged, leaning down, and planting warm kisses on her neck up to her mouth as he captured her lips in a slow sensual kiss. Pulling away, he met her dreamy gaze and said, "It's such a cool, crisp day today and so pretty out there. How about after breakfast, we bundle up, go outside and let Prairie and Stetson out into the pasture to play in the snow?"

MJ's lips curled up into a smile as she glanced towards the view outside their bedroom window. "I'd love that."

* * *

KOLT COULDN'T WAIT another day without asking her. He had mistakenly thought that proposing would be easy. Just find a special moment and do it. The truth was that he had waited so long for Jane that no moment felt special enough. Jane deserved something over the top and incredible, but when he woke this morning and saw his girl looking so beautiful in the white glow from the snow outside their window. As he watched her marvel at the simplicity of nature's beauty, and relished the calm of the quiet morning, he realized it didn't matter how or when. Jane didn't care about the details. All she wanted was to spend her life with him as much as he wanted to spend his life with her. So here he was, the ring sitting loose in his pocket, his fingers finding it again and again as they trudged through the snow from the house to the barn. Just the knowledge that it was there in his pocket and what it meant brought such a deep sense of awareness. He swallowed hard, tamping down his nervousness, hoping he had the right words at the moment. The right words to express all that he wanted to say.

Reaching the barn, Jane made her way to Prairie's box stall, and, as usual, he was there to greet her with a snort, a whinny and his perked-up ears. If a horse could smile, there was no question that he was smiling at Jane.

"Good morning, sweet boy," she said, entering his box stall and wrapping her arms around his neck in a careful hug. She was cautious with him, and although the gunshot wound was healed over, the large gnarly scar was a stark reminder of what they had been through. She gingerly ran her fingers over the raised skin, and leaned in, kissing the scar, Prairie pressing in as she did. "I love you." She said, smoothing her hands over his muzzle and giving him an affectionate scratch. Prairie responded, trying to nip at the pompom on her toque, making her giggle. The sweet sound bounced off the walls and made Kolt chuckle.

Kolt smiled wistfully, setting a lead rope over the side of the stall for Jane to use as he made his way over to Stetson's box stall next to Prairie's. Entering his stall, he showered a little love on his horse too, with Stetson leaning in and accepting his scratches with pleasure. Clipping the lead rope to his halter, he guided Stetson out of the stall, with Jane and Prairie already in the aisle waiting for them. Leading their horses towards the back entrance of the barn, they stomped through the shallow drifts of snow to reach the pasture gate. Opening the gate, they led their horses inside and unclipped their lead ropes. Kolt turned to lock the gate, and when he turned back, both Prairie and Stetson had taken off running through the freshly fallen snow. Prairie fell to his side and rolled around on his back, covering himself with the white powder, and Jane peeled with delighted laughter, clapping her mittened hands and making Kolt melt at the unbridled joy on her face as she watched their horses.

Kolt approached, wrapping his arms around her from behind and kissing her cheek. Jane leaned in and let out a happy sigh as she said, "So this is what true happiness is."

Kolt smiled, kissing her head with affection, as he replied. "It is, Pretty Girl, but I know how I can make you even happier."

"How is that possible?" she giggled, turning to face him, his hands holding hers. "You, Kolt, have made every dream I could dare to dream come true. You have made me so happy; I don't know if it's possible to be happier than this."

"Is that a challenge?" he asked, cocking a playful brow at her as his lips curled into his endearing lopsided grin. "I know one way I can make you the happiest woman in Primrose."

She giggled again, swatting him on the chest playfully with her mittened hand before she met his gaze, now earnest as he dropped to one knee right there in the snow. Looking up at the woman he loved more than life itself, his heart full to bursting he said, "From the moment I met you, you had me, and I knew that day that I could search my whole life through and never find another you. I love you, Jane, and I would be honored and humbled if you would marry me." He reached into his pocket, pulled out a vintage diamond solitaire, and met her gaze, now brimming with tears of joy as he held it out to her. "Will you marry me, Pretty Girl, and spend the rest of your life with me?"

Without a moment of hesitation, her answer burst from her lips, "Yes! Yes! A thousand times yes!"

With an "aww shucks" grin, and tears of happiness in

his eyes, he slipped off her mitten and slid the ring on her finger, bringing her hand to his lips and pressing a sweet kiss to her ring. She leaned down, taking his face in her hands and captured his lips in a passionate kiss. As their lips met, Prairie's whinny echoed across the field, making them break their kiss and turn their heads toward him.

Off in the distance, Prairie stood still, proudly watching them, snow kissing his coat, the winter wind blowing his tail and mane in long wild wisps. Prairie whinnied again, and Kolt rose to his feet, raising his chin in acknowledgement as he shouted back, "You've done good, Prairie Prestige. I got her now." Prairie's stance eased, and with one last look, he galloped away carefree, fading into a cloud of swirling snow.

JANE GLANCED up at Ben as he fiddled with the collar of his white shirt, messing up the fold over his suit jacket and the alignment of his bow tie.

"Ben, stop messing with your collar and tie." Ever scolded with a laugh as she reached up straightening them, and he leaned down stealing a chaste kiss.

"I just want to look good for this wedding. No one has ever asked me to walk them down the aisle before," he said, giving Jane a quick wink.

"I think you look handsome, Ben," Jane said, looking up at him with affection from her seat at the Donahue kitchen table as Whitney put the finishing touches on her hair.

A sweet newborn cry sounded from the bassinet close

by, and she rose, striding over and leaning down to pick up her two-month-old son, Gatton Patrick Donahue. "Awake just in time." She cooed, bringing him over her shoulder and patting his tiny bottom as she rubbed his back in gentle circles, inhaling his sweet baby powder scent.

"Let me change him and feed him a bottle before we go." Emmaline Donahue offered, reaching for her newborn grandson. "You go get your dress on. If I know my son, he's probably already pacing in that meadow waiting for you."

Jane smiled; she couldn't wait to see him too. Choosing to stick to tradition and not see each other before they walked down the aisle had proven difficult, and she missed him terribly. There wasn't a night since she had moved in with him that she hadn't fallen asleep in his arms, and not a single morning that he didn't wake her with his ticklish stubble and sweet caresses. That was until last night.

As if reading her mind, Whitney took in her bereft look and put her hand on her shoulder. "Let's get you to your cowboy," she said as Whitney, Ever and Georgie guided her up the stairs to their room.

With their help, she slipped into the intricate dress she had picked out for their special day. The dress was completely lace, with a fitted curve-hugging bodice, thin straps over her shoulders plunging to an open back that dipped to her waist. The skirt was full, with the satin underlay kissing the ground and the lace overlay cascading past the hemline in a delicate train.

"You look incredible." Whitney complimented her

with tears in her eyes as she blinked rapidly trying to keep them at bay. "All week I've been thinking back to when you first came to Primrose. Remembering you then and seeing you now, about to marry your handsome cowboy, it reminds me that fate has a funny way of bringing us full circle."

Fate had brought them full circle. A year ago, she was running, scared, scarred, a shell of the woman standing here in this gorgeous dress ready to marry the man of her dreams. A man who taught her to trust and helped her to heal; showed her what true unconditional love felt like. The hand of God, fate, destiny, whatever you wanted to call it, had brought her and Kolt together and reminded them both that good things were worth waiting for.

"You, Jane, have made my brother so happy. I hope someday I'll find that kind of love." Georgie said wistfully. Ever reached for Georgie's hand, giving it a reassuring squeeze as she reached for Whitney's hand, and MJ took Whitney and Georgie's in hers. An unbreakable circle of support connected them.

"I know you and Kolt have been through so much, and you two have proven to be beyond strong, but I do have some simple advice for you as an old married woman." Ever said with a wink as her expression turned reflective. "Just love each other. Every day, no matter what the day brings, reach for each other. If you do that, you will have a happy marriage like Ben and I and like Whitney and Hayden share."

MJ looked between the women in the circle, feeling immense gratitude fill her chest. *These are my sisters.* Their bond was one of family. Blinking back tears, she pulled them in for a group hug, feeling every ounce of love and support from these strong women.

"No crying!" Whitney exclaimed, dabbing a tear from her cheek as they broke their embrace. "This is a joyous day! Let's get you married!"

* * *

KOLT ROCKED in his cowboy boots anxiously under their oak tree in front of the wooden trellis cascading with wildflowers and greenery. He glanced over to the hitching post Hayden built and took in Prairie and Stetson, fully saddled and watching as the guests filed in, taking their seats on wooden benches flagged with thick logs to brace them. At the end of each row was a wrought iron hook holding a mason jar with a menagerie of brightly colored wildflowers tied with thick yellow ribbons. The décor was natural and beautiful. Just like his bride.

His bride. How he waited to say those words. Jane was so much more than he could have imagined for himself. Not only was she the most beautiful, sweet, kind and brave woman he had ever met, but she was also unshakably strong, her 20 hours of labor attesting to it. She had been stoic, a warrior, and when she mustered the strength for that final push and his son's cry sounded in the delivery room he met her eyes, so full of joyful tears that he knew then and there that he could never, and would never, love or admire anyone more.

Today, before God and all their family and friends, he could finally declare her, his. Lost in his daydreams he heard the gentle strum of the guitar start as his mother walked down the aisle, cradling little Gatton, all scrunched up in his tiny suit pants, white shirt, suspenders and bow tie, his light dusting of blonde hair shimmering in the summer sun. Reaching the front of the aisle, his mother brought his newborn son over to him, and he leaned down, planting a kiss on his sweet head before she took a seat in the front row.

Georgie, Whitney and Ever followed all dressed in flowy yellow knee length sundresses and holding bouquets of colorful wildflowers tied up with yellow ribbons, their faces beaming as they lined up opposite Kolt, Hayden at his side as his best man, along with Thatcher Stevens and Brooks Isley.

The guitar instrumental changed to a familiar tune, a song he had requested be played for this moment and knew was sentimental to Jane. A tribute to her grandparents. "The Yellow Rose of Texas" drifted on the breeze as his eyes floated to the end of the aisle and his breath caught. So close but so far away was his Pretty Girl, her arm looped through the hulking arm of his dear friend and Jane's father figure, Ben. They slowly made their way down the aisle, her hazel eyes locked on him, Ben's chin up high, prouder than he had ever seen. As she approached, he could fully take in her beauty, and it made him breathless. The dress was stunning, accentuating her curvy body to perfection, but the woman wearing it eclipsed the radiant sun that shone down on them. He had never seen anyone more beautiful.

The minister stepped forward, holding a Bible in his hand as Jane and Ben reached the end of the aisle, and he asked. "Who gives this woman to this man?"

"I do." Ben replied, his baritone deep and sure as he turned and engulfed her in a hug. Jane giggled as he released her, and Kolt stepped forward. Ben placed her hand in his, giving Kolt a death stare and growl under his breath like a bear.

"You be good to her, Donahue," he warned with a slow grin tugging at his lips and his eyes crinkling with his smile.

Kolt nodded, letting out a chuckle and clapping Ben on the shoulder.

Her hand in his, he led her to the trellis, and they turned to face each other, taking each other's hands as he said, "You have me speechless again, Pretty Girl. So beautiful."

"You like?" she asked, twisting her hips to make the skirt swish.

"I love," he replied, looking her up and down as his eyes drifted back to hers. "I love you."

She beamed brightly, her eyes shining with happiness as the minister spoke. "Welcome everyone to the wedding ceremony uniting Mary Jane Kasper and Koltson Donahue. Now I have been given direct instructions by the Groom to keep this short and sweet as Kolt told me he has waited for 36 years to marry the woman of his dreams and he doesn't want to wait another minute to lock this down." the minister said, holding his hands up in the air. "Those were Kolt's words, not mine."

Chuckles and amens sounded from the guests, making both Kolt and Jane laugh as the minister went on. "As much as the groom wants to get this show on the road, I wouldn't be doing my job if I didn't leave you with some words of wisdom from the gospel." he said, raising his bible in the air for all to see. "Kolt and Jane have been very open and honest with me about their story, and now as I see them here before me, there is one sentence from 1 John Chapter 4 that says it simply: "There is no fear in love." It goes on to say that "love drives out fear." These two souls have been on a journey to get here. A journey that was difficult and full of uncertainty and fear. But they loved each other through it all, and their steadfast love drove out the fear. Today they come before us fearless and ready for the next part of their lives together. May God bless them on their journey." Amens sounded from the guests as the minister nodded to Kolt to go ahead with his vows.

Reaching into his pocket, Kolt pulled out a piece of paper, slowly opening it as his gaze met his bride's, emotion brimming on the edge. "I've always believed in love. Have been surrounded by it, having the best example with my parents," he said, turning to his mother first, then looking up and pointing to the heavens. "I always believed I would eventually find it, but never did I think it would find me at a roadside rest stop," he said with a low laugh, making her smile grow wider. "From the moment I saw you, I knew I was a goner. I don't believe that two souls find each other by simple accident. I truly believe God brought you to me," he said, brushing a tear from his cheek. "Jane, you are the one I want to wake up with every morning and the one I want to ride into the sunset with every night. I want to raise a family with you, build a farm with you, right here in this meadow, and spend the rest of my life loving you. I love you, Pretty Girl. Today, tomorrow and always."

Tears streaked down Jane's face, and Kolt reached into his pocket for a handkerchief, dabbing her cheeks, their rosy hue so beautiful in the shade of their oak tree. Taking a deep breath, she let out a long exhale and bent down, pulling up the front of her skirt to reveal her dusty brown cowboy boots, her hand dipping into one to pull out a piece of paper. The guests chuckled as she held out the paper for everyone to see, and Kolt shook his head with a laugh.

"Kolt, my love. There are so many things I feel as I look into your eyes right now. So many words like gratitude, happiness and love come to mind, but there is one word that always sticks out above the rest when I look at you." Jane paused; her eyes locked on his as she said. "Home. And I don't mean a place to lay our heads down at night, or a town like Primrose even though I do consider it my hometown now." She said as she turned to their guests, to be met by a few whoops. "Wherever you are, Kolt is where I want to be. You are my shelter from the storm, my rock and my foundation. You, Kolt, are my home. I love you, RC, today, tomorrow and always."

Reaching over, he caressed her cheek tenderly, and drawing her closer, he leaned in, eyes locked, their foreheads touching. The minister cleared his throat, and they turned their heads to him. "Almost there," he said with an amused grin. "Rings, please."

Hayden handed over the rings, and the minister blessed them, handing one to Kolt, then gesturing for him to go ahead.

"I, Koltson Donahue, take you, Mary Jane Kasper, to be my wife. To love and to cherish through good times and in bad until death do us part," he pledged as he slipped a simple gold band onto her finger.

The minister handed Jane a ring, and she took Kolt's hand as she vowed, "I, Mary Jane Kasper, take you, Koltson Donahue, to be my husband. To love and to cherish through good times and in bad until death do us part." With her words, she slipped the ring on his finger and beamed up at him excitedly.

"Then it is my pleasure to pronounce by the Church of Christ that you are officially married. Kolt, you may kiss your bride."

"Finally!" he exclaimed, pulling her close, his large hand coming around the back of her neck, his other at the small of her back as he suddenly dipped her, making her squeak, then throw her head back in a joyous giggle.

"Kolt!" she chided playfully as he kissed up her exposed neck to her lips and captured her in a passionate kiss in front of God and all their family and friends. The guests rose, whistled and whooped as he brought her back to her feet and steadied her, kissing her again before they turned to their guests.

"For the first time, Kolt and Jane Donahue!" the minister exclaimed, as their guests stood and cheered.

Kolt turned his gaze to Jane and cocked an eyebrow at her in question. She smiled and nodded her answer as they turned, Ben and Georgie having untied Prairie and Stetson from the hitching post. Kolt accepted the reins from Georgie and mounted his horse while Jane followed with Ben's help and straightened the skirt of her dress as they turned their horses west towards the setting sun. Reaching across the gap between their horses, Kolt took her hand, giving it a gentle squeeze as he asked, "Are you ready to ride off into the sunset with me, Mrs. Donahue?"

"Forever and always."

With all their loved ones watching, they rode off with the sun making its farewell descent and painting vibrant colors in the glorious prairie sky. Two fateful souls having found each other and riding towards their bright and beautiful future.

EPILOGUE

Five years later in the Fall

"Gatton, can you please take your brother's hand?" MJ asked as she stepped out onto the porch of their farmhouse, holding a large wooden salad bowl. "I don't want Nash to trip on the stairs."

"Okay, Mommy," her sweet, blonde-haired, brown-eyed 5-year-old son said as he took his 2-year-old brother's chubby little hand.

"Good man." Kolt praised, ruffling Gatton's mop of hair as he climbed the stairs quickly, coming to her side. "I'm more worried about you tripping on these stairs, Pretty Girl."

Giving him a grateful look, she handed Kolt the salad bowl and took his arm. "I can't see my feet anymore." She said with a frown as she clutched her huge baby belly and slowly descended the stairs.

"Not much longer." Kolt reassured with his brows knit together in concern for his wife. *Not much longer*, she repeated in her head. 38 weeks pregnant, this being her third pregnancy, it had been harder than she expected. Chasing after two rambunctious boys while watching your body balloon and feet swell up to double the size was not for the faint of heart. But soon it would be over, and she knew, like the two times before, she would miss this stage as she held her newborn in her arms.

Waddling across the lawn, MJ took in the scene and grinned. All their closest friends and family were in attendance, and a long wooden family-style table stretched across the width of the yard, framed by wooden chairs. The table was simple and elegant with mason jars of fall flowers and set in between eclectic place settings of rich orange, brown, yellow and red. Delicious smelling food covered every open surface, each guest bringing their specialty to share for their annual Friendsgiving Potluck dinner. A tradition started the year they were married, bringing all the people they were most grateful for together every year.

"This all looks so amazing." She said, taking in the scene and reaching for Kolt's hand. "Can you gather everyone, RC?"

"Dinner's ready!" Kolt shouted as everyone turned, making their way to the table. The sweet sounds of conversation and laughter drifted over the yard as everyone took their seats. Kolt took his place at the head of the table, and MJ sat next to him, flanked by their young sons. Once everyone was settled, Kolt stood from the table, commanding everyone's attention and quieting the crowd. "Before we dig into this amazing looking food, I wanted to share a few things that I'm thankful for this Thanksgiving. Firstly, I'm thankful to all of you, our wonderful family, and friends. Family doesn't always have to be blood, and I think this group has proven that," he said, as everyone turned to each other with nods of understanding. "I'm thankful for this farm, which was only a dream five years ago and now is our homestead. I'm thankful for continued health," he said, his voice thick with emotion as his eyes drifted to where his sister Georgie sat with Brooks' arm around her protectively. She met his gaze, her eyes shiny with tears as she gave him a nod of acknowledgement. "I'm thankful for my two sons and my daughter, who could arrive any day now," he said, placing his hand on MJ's burgeoning belly. "And lastly, I'm thankful for my beautiful wife, whom, if it is actually possible, I love more today than the day I married her," he said, turning to face her and reaching for her hand. "I thank God every day for bringing you into my life. I love you so much, Pretty Girl."

"I love you too, RC," Jane replied as he leaned down and brushed his lips tenderly to hers.

"Okay, enough of this mushy stuff," Thatcher exclaimed. "Let's pray and dig into this amazing food."

Everyone bowed their heads in prayer, Ben taking the lead as was tradition, and when a resounding "Amen" echoed through the guests, it was followed quickly by swelled chatter and laughter along with the clatter of dishes being passed around the table. As everyone enjoyed the food and fellowship, MJ smiled ardently at the joy and love around this family table. Each person played a part, whether it be big or small, in her journey to get here. With a heart full of gratitude for these people, this farm, this town, her children, and the love of the man next to her, she looked towards the sky and breathed out towards the heavens, *Thank you.*

* * *

Thank you for reading Prairie Prestige!
Want more steamy romance set in the idyllic small town
of Primrose?
Read Prairie Roads now!

ALSO BY TANYA RENEE

Primrose Series

Prairie Sky

Prairie Nights

Prairie Fire

Prairie Hearts

Prairie Sound

Prairie Rain

Prairie Prestige

Prairie Roads

With The Band

Finding Direction

Love Notes

On The Edge Of Forever

The Spring of Love Series

By Virginia Taylor

Forever Delighted

Forever Amused

Forever Heartfelt

The Tooth Fairy Chronicles

By Victoria Rocus

Tooth Decay With A Side Of Fae

Toothaches And Wedding Cakes

Baby Tooth And Tangled Roots

Wisdom Tooth And The Awful Truth

Missing Teeth And What Lies Beneath

Toothless Grins And His Father's Sins

For more information visit:

www.serenadepublishing.com

ABOUT THE AUTHOR

Tanya Renee is a proud Canadian Prairie girl, who grew up on a family farm in Southeastern Manitoba Canada. Always an avid reader, she became intrigued with the romance genre at an early age when she first read Romeo and Juliet. Soon after she started to craft her own stories and poetry and by the time she was in high school, she had declared someday she would become a writer.

Married to the love of her life, she resides in Steinbach, Manitoba Canada with two teenagers and a menagerie of pets. When she's not cooking up a storm in her kitchen, she can be found tinkering in her garden, drinking copious amounts of coffee with a book in hand, listening to 80's music/audio books or at her laptop creating stories that are emotionally satisfying. She writes what she wants to read, epic stories that bring you on a journey and make you believe in love.

www.tanyareneeromance.com

ACKNOWLEDGMENTS

There are so many people I could thank for inspiring this novel, so, I will start with my biggest inspiration, my dad. A man who has a profound love of horses, farming and worked beyond hard to support our family. A man who gave myself, my sister and brother a memorable childhood. Many of those memories and little easter eggs about my childhood finding their way into this novel and others. So many memories of weekends spent attending horse shows, fairs and rodeos watching him and my sister compete. Watching proudly as they took home ribbon after ribbon. Trophy after trophy. Dad, through seeing you pursue your passions you taught me to follow mine. To work hard, never give up and always work hard to reach my potential. I am forever grateful for the lessons you've taught me. Love you.

Secondly, I want to thank my sister, Jennifer. A true equestrian talent and the inspiration for the horse show scene in this novel. Reliving memories of you competing through my research, watching video after video of Western Pleasure and showmanship classes, remembering how excited I was when you placed. Seeing firsthand the unspoken connection between rider and horse. Following you and your success has shown me the power of persistence and tenacity. You are incredible. Never forget that.

Next, I need to thank my mom, who other than my husband has to be my biggest fan on this writing journey. I hope I make you proud with this story. Thank you for your unfailing support!

To my husband and kids who have ridden this wild ride alongside me. You three are my rock and my sanctuary. I love you all.

To my amazingly loyal and committed readers. As promised, here's your cowboy romance! I hope you fall in love with Kolt Donahue as much as I have. Trust me, this is not the last cowboy you'll meet in Primrose. Stay tuned for more! You are the best!

And lastly, to Sarah Williams, the CEO of Serenade Publishing. I can't put into words how grateful I am every day that my stories have found their home with Serenade Publishing. You make dreams come true. Thank you for believing in me!